The Swinger's Club: Tiffany and I

By Zoe Waters

Cover art by Lies Thru a Lens

Table of Contents:

The Swinger's Club: Tiffany and Liam ….. page 1

The Swinger's Club: Chad and Lexi ….. page 43

The Swinger's Club: Amanda Worthington ….. page 87

The Swinger's Club: Natalie Smyth ….. page 140

The Swinger's Club: Tiffany and Liam

As I stepped into The Swinger's Club, a wave of relief hit me. It's taken two years of planning to make this night happen. A part of me thought this moment would never come.

I looked over at my husband, Liam, and gave his hand a squeeze. All my subtle manipulations have finally paid off. All the planning Jay and I did has culminated in this night. We were finally at The Swinger's Club.

#####

When I was in grade ten, I met Jay Block. His wavy black hair, broad chest, and eyes that pierced right through you when he looked your way drew me in. Before he even spoke to me, I'd fallen. Hard. It took me six months to get up the nerve to tell him I liked him as more than a friend. In reply, he broke my heart as he said, "Angie and I are going steady. I wish you would've said something last week as I like you, too."

I mourned what could've been with a week of tears before making myself get out of bed and rejoin reality.

Colin came into my life a few months later and we started going steady. A month later, Angie dumped Jay for one of his friends. I let him cry on my shoulder but I didn't give up the security of Colin for a chance with Jay.

We all graduated from high school. I spent the summer working to save money for my upcoming stint at the University of California. Things with Colin were starting to fizzle out. I cared for him but he wasn't the love of my life. Two days before I left for Los Angeles, I broke up with Colin. He wasn't upset. He claimed he was ready to move on, too. That chapter was happily closed.

The next day, the night before I left for L.A., my three closest girlfriends and I went out for pizza. Jay was there with a group of his friends. All nine of us ended up sitting together, reminiscing about the past years and pondering how the future looked. When the night was winding down, Jay insisted that he walk me to my car.

"Colin isn't going to know what to do with himself once you leave," Jay said; he'd never been Colin's #1 fan.

"He'll be fine. We broke up yesterday."

"Oh no," Jay said with no conviction. "Are you okay?"

"I'm fine. We probably should've split a long time ago."

"I agree with that. Like two years ago when Angie and I split."

"Probably," I replied, although I hated to even consider that I'd wasted my time with Colin.

Jay took my hand as we crossed the parking lot. He brought it up to his face and kissed each of my fingers. A flock of butterflies took flight deep in my gut.

When we reached my blue Ford Festiva, Jay took my keys. He unlocked the driver's door and held it open until I was inside. He walked around to the passenger side and let himself in. Sitting side by side, we looked at each other in silence for a few moments before Jay spoke. "We have never had good timing, you and I. I blame myself for that."

"It's not your fault," I insisted. "It's just the way things worked out."

"I disagree. Had we tried harder, we could've given us a real shot."

I was about to disagree again when Jeff held up his hand to stop me. "It doesn't matter now," he said. "It's a moot point. And with you off to L.A. tomorrow, this is not the right time to start something, I know."

"You're right." As much as I liked Jay and had lusted after him for years, I wasn't up for the challenges of a long-distance relationship at that point in my life.

"You never know what'll happen in four years, if you come back," he said.

"Let's flip that around. Who knows where you'll be." That was said out of kindness. Jay and I both knew that with his family ties and obligations, he wouldn't venture far. Jay laughed, knowing I was being kind.

A blanket of electric tension settled over us. It was time to say good-bye but neither of us wanted to make the first move.

"You'll stay in touch, won't you?" Jay asked.

"You know I will. And you better write me back."

"I will."

"Good. Well, I should get going," I said, although booting Jay out of my car was the last thing I wanted to do.

"Before you go, can I ask you one favor?"

"Of course. Anything." There wasn't much I would deny him.

"I've always wondered what it would be like to kiss you. May I?"

The butterflies in my gut turned into a stampede of buffalo. I swallowed deeply and managed to reply, "Sure." I'd dreamt of the same thing for over two years and couldn't believe it was going to happen.

I leaned slightly toward Jay and he closed the rest of the distance between us. There was no easing into the kiss; his mouth devoured mine the second we touched. I couldn't breathe as his tongue probed my mouth but I didn't care. After the initial shock was over, I responded with gusto. My tongue searched every crevice in his mouth as my hands snaked up his arms and into his hair.

When Jay's hands slid under my t-shirt and unclasped my bra, I didn't stop him. My bra loose and hanging away from my body, Jay grasped at my bare breasts. The groan that echoed between our mouths startled me when I realized it came from my throat.

The moment was turning heavy. Making out had never felt like this with Colin. My skin had never been electrified where he'd touched it. Every inch Jay brushed was left with a scorched imprint.

Jay leaned over me and pulled the handle that reclined my seat. Our kiss broke as I fell backward. Jay's lips moved to my neck and traveled from one side to the other. My hands remained buried in his hair, my fingertips memorizing every ridge on his head.

Jay inched my shirt up until it was bunched around my collarbone. His lips moved from my neck to my chest. He took my left nipple in his mouth. He rolled the nipple around his tongue and nibbled on it until it was achingly hard. Only then did he move to my right nipple, where he did the same thing.

My body was melting into the seat. My bones were turning to mush and I was in danger of losing all semblance of control over my body and thoughts. I was more than okay with that!

Jay's mouth stayed on my chest as his hands trailed down my stomach to play with the snap on my shorts. Through the haze that was fogging up my brain, I felt his hard cock pressing against the side of my thigh. One of my hands left his hair and aimed for his hardness. I squeezed him over his jeans and felt his throbbing even through the denim.

My core was pulsating, too. I was wet and ready for action, my pussy eager for what I was clutching. I grabbed Jay's wrist and shoved his hand down my shorts. His fingers slid into my wetness as one of them struck my clit, driving me wild.

Just when I was about to lose control, Jay's hand froze in my core and his head pulled free of my chest. "Whoa, whoa, whoa," he said, although I wasn't sure if he was talking to himself or me.

"What?" I asked. I could tell he wanted me as much as I was aching for him; his hard-on didn't lie.

"We can't do this," he said.

A bolt of anger hit me. *We can't do this*. What the hell did that mean? I reached for his cock again, giving him another squeeze through his jeans. "You want it, too," I said, desperate for him.

Jay pulled his hand from my shorts and took a hold of my arm, moving it away from his crotch. "I want you more than I've ever wanted anyone in my life. But I respect you too much to screw you in a parking lot behind a pizza joint with people wandering by."

"I don't care," I spat, my anger at being denied overriding my other emotions.

"No," he insisted. "This isn't happening. You leave tomorrow for four years. Four years! It would kill me to make love to you now and then have to watch you walk out of my life tomorrow."

"What the hell are you talking about? This has nothing to do with tomorrow! It's about the next ten minutes, nothing more."

Jay opened his door and stepped outside. The cool air hit me like a wall after we'd steamed things up inside the car; the fresh air instantly cleared my head.

I redid up my bra, straightened my clothes, and climbed out of the car. Jay was pacing the empty parking stalls, his hands racing through his hair. The look of angst on his face erased every iota of anger that had been consuming me moments before. I walked over to where he stood and hugged him, my arms tightening around him so he couldn't push me away. But he didn't even try. He wrapped his arms around me, his lips pressing against my forehead.

We stood that way for many minutes, long enough for us both to simmer down.

A car pulled into the stall next to us, breaking into the bubble we'd created around ourselves. Jay pulled back and looked at me. "You okay?" he asked.

I nodded. "You?"

"I'm okay. I'm sorry I let things get that far."

"Please don't apologize. It degrades what happened in my car."

Jay cupped my jaw with his hands, forcing me to look at him. "Don't twist my words, baby. We're both on edge. Let me be clear about one thing. I want to make love to you more than you will ever know. But it's not going to happen tonight with you leaving tomorrow. I wouldn't recover. I love and respect you too much for that. Do not leave here thinking I don't want you."

I gulped. "Okay."

Jay bent slightly to kiss me, a soft meeting of our lips that conveyed even more than his words had said. When we broke apart, Jay dropped his hands from my face and walked to my car. He opened the driver's door and I turtle-walked to him, dragging out having to say good-bye. My heart was breaking.

Jay took me in his arms one more time, hugging me so tight we must have looked like one person to anyone walking by. He pulled away first, gently manoeuvring me into my car. "Stay in touch," he said as he shut my door.

I rolled down my window. "I will. I'll miss you."

"I'll miss you more than you can imagine." He gave me a quick peck through the window before he turned and walked to his car.

I watched him, my heart aching more with each step he took. As he drove away, Jay looked at me one last time. His face conveyed nothing but pain. His car vanished around the corner and I felt like he'd taken a piece of me with him. We'd been robbed, Jay and I. It may not have been a rational thought but that was how I felt.

I left for school the next day with a storm cloud hanging over my head and threatening to let loose. But life went on, as it does. As I grew more immersed in university life, I thought of Jay a tiny bit less with each passing day. I knew we'd have our moment together eventually and that knowledge kept me going.

But that fantasy was shattered in the middle of my junior year when I heard through the rumor mill that Jay had gotten a girl pregnant and was going to marry her. I mourned for what could've been but I didn't give in to the urge to wallow in my pain.

Life continued. I graduated and moved to Chicago where I joined an architecture firm. That was where I met Liam a few years later. He walked into my office, a new client, and it hit me how lonely I'd been. I let him wine and dine me and after a suitable number of dates, I let him take me to bed. While fireworks didn't go off, I was satisfied and that was enough for me. So when Liam asked me to marry him a year later, I said yes. We eloped to Bermuda where we tied the knot on the beach at sunset. It was the perfect start to our lives together.

We bought a bigger apartment together and merged our lives together. Years passed as we both climbed the corporate ladder. Our lives outside of work were content.

A kink was thrown into our comfortable lives when I opened Facebook one night to find a friend request from Jay Block. Just seeing his name caused a bolt of excited trepidation to race through me. Excitement was quickly replaced with disgust; I was annoyed with myself that Jay still had the power to cause such a strong reaction in me.

Before I had the sense to question if I was making the right decision or not, I hit 'accept.' I was granted immediate access to Jay's life. I scrolled through his list of friends and recognized a few names from high school. His status had him as married and I creeped his wife, Sherry Block. She was vaguely familiar. As I looked through her pictures, I clued in that she went to the same high school as Jay and I but she was a year behind us. They had three children and their life looked like a Norman Rockwell painting. A pang of pain hit me. Liam and I hadn't had any luck so far in the children department.

I was scrolling through Jay's pictures when a chat box popped up at the bottom of the screen. *Hey Tiffany.* It was Jay.

*Jay! Hi, how are you?* I answered before I panicked and signed off Facebook.

*I'm good. How are you?*

*I'm good, too. I'm a bit surprised to hear from you though, to be honest.*

*I'll bet. Facebook suggested we be friends so I took their advice.*

I laughed. That was such a Jay thing to say. We spent the next hour catching up on the past decade. As the rumor mill had said, Jay had knocked up his girlfriend and ended up marrying her.

Before we said goodnight, we promised each other we'd stay in touch.

As I lay in bed that night next to Liam, I pondered what good would come from being in touch with Jay. Maybe nothing but I had missed having him in my life.

We chatted a couple of times a month as the year passed, mainly catching up on the details of our lives and what was currently going on with us. Our chats were a nice reprieve in a life that I hadn't realized I needed a reprieve from.

Ten months after we became Facebook friends, Jay threw me into a tailspin in one of our chats. *Hey, Tiff. What are you doing this Saturday night?*

I checked my calendar app. *Nothing. Why?*

*I'm going to be in Chicago for work. Want to spend the night with me?*

Whoa! What the hell was that invite? *'Spend the night' as in spend the night?*

*Yes. My hotel room. Aren't we due for our shot? Even if it's only one night?*

I'd never cheated on Liam. I'd never pondered any option other than being faithful but now Jay had thrown one in my face. To buy myself time to think, I messaged *Is your wife okay with that?*

*Sherry wouldn't know.*

*Are sleepovers with women something you do regularly?*

*I wouldn't say regularly. A few times over the years. Sherry is such a dud in bed. She hates it when I touch her anymore.*

*That makes it okay?*

*I didn't say that. I miss you and think of you all the time. I regret not making love to you that night in your Festiva.*

*I regret that, too, but that doesn't mean I'll cheat on my husband.*

*The bastard is a lucky guy.*

*Yes he is.* After a pause, I typed, *I'll pass on Saturday night but thanks for the offer.*

*Text me if you change your mind.* He gave me his cell number, which I put in my phone under the name 'Sherry' to remind me that he was married.

We signed off shortly after that.

As much as I didn't want to think about Jay's proposal, that was uppermost in my mind every day leading up to the weekend. It was even worse on Saturday. Just knowing that Jay was in the same city as me had my body aching for him. I remembered his touch like we'd been making out in my car yesterday.

Every minute that night was agony. It was excruciatingly difficult not to text Jay and ask what hotel he was at. But I managed to stay strong and I ignored my cell phone.

I let a week pass before I texted Jay. *Did you have fun in Chicago?*

*No. It was miserable being so close to you but not close at all.*

*I felt the same.* That wasn't easy to admit to Jay but one thing about us was that we'd always been upfront and honest with one another.

*What's it going to take for me to get you in the sack?*

He had such sweet pillow talk - not! *Sherry to occupy Liam would do it.* I replied, more as a joke than a real answer, as I didn't have a real answer.

Jay didn't reply for a couple of hours, which wasn't like him when we were in the midst of a conversation. I texted him - *Did I offend you with what I said? I was just joking.* Jay didn't offend easily so that likely wasn't it; I had no idea why he suddenly went quiet.

*Hold tight.*

I did as he suggested, working hard to not give him another thought until he texted me the next day. *What if we could make that happen?*

*Sherry and Liam?*

*Yes. If so, then you and I would be a go?*

The thought of Sherry and Liam together was an odd one but I'd be willing to have that happen if it meant Jay and I got to finish what we started all those years ago. *Yes, we'd be a go. But how is that going to pan out?*

*I did some digging. There is a swinger's club in Chicago called, appropriately enough, The Swinger's Club. The four of us would go the same night and you and I will make sure we end up together. Sherry and Liam would go off to do their thing and you and I would go find ourselves a private corner.*

Fuck me sideways! Where had that come from? I could barely process what Jay had suggested. There were such places as swinger's clubs? They weren't just inventions for cheesy Hollywood movies? When I recovered from the shock, I messaged Jay back - *Have you ever been to a swinger's club?*

*No, as you need to go as a couple.*

*How do we convince Sherry and Liam to do this?*

*Carefully. Slowly over the next few months, we bring up swinging and plant the seed. And watch it grow. When the time is right, we point out the upsides and pick a date.*

That was exactly what Jay and I did. He worked on Sherry while I planted the idea in a tiny corner of Liam's thoughts. Months passed. I hit a roadblock with Liam. Jay gave me pointers on how to bypass the hurdle; movies to watch together that featured swinging in a positive light, things to say to boost his sexual ego, how to casually point out other women without being obvious. It worked. A new year rolled around and I thought Liam was ready for me to approach the idea of a night at the swinger's club with him. I'd rehearsed the conversation with Jay a half dozen times by that point. I was ready.

Timing was crucial. I made his favorite dinner - veal cutlets and baby potatoes - and broached the subject with confidence, as Jay had suggested. "Have you ever thought of swinging?" I asked.

Liam finished chewing what was in his mouth and washed it down with a swig of Merlot.

"Not really. Why?" He didn't appear outraged by my question, a good start.

"My boss at work was telling me about a swingers club in town that she and her hubby went to. She said it was a lot of fun." That was the story Jay and I had come up with.

"Oh yeah?"

"Yeah. She said it spiced up their sex life."

Liam's jaw clenched. "You think our sex life needs spicing up?"

"I think there isn't any couple's sex life that couldn't benefit from a little extra spice."

"Why don't we go to the adult shop you eyeball every time we drive by it? We can find some spicy toys in there, I would wager."

*Tread carefully*, I warned myself. This was the make or break moment. "I thought of that. I can't help but think of how much fun Janice had with her husband going to the club. Shall I invite them to dinner one night to share the story of their experience?"

I was gambling that he'd say no; Janice was the biggest unknown in this conversation. She hadn't actually been to a swinger's club as far as I knew.

I breathed a massive sigh of relief under my breath when Liam said, "No, that's okay." After a pause, Liam asked, "Is that something you really want to do?"

I pretended to ponder his question. After a suitable amount of time had passed, I replied, "I think it could be fun. We can just hang out and watch, too. We don't have to do anything. If we go and it turns out to not be our thing, we can leave without doing anything."

Liam mulled that over. "Okay. Let's give it a try."

I worked hard not to jump up and down and cheer like a spastic schoolgirl. "I'll check with Janice on how it works.

Then you and I can pin down a date to go. I'll check with the club's availability, too, and figure out how that works."

"Sounds good." Our conversation then morphed into other topics - the new president, the rising cost of groceries, and the debate over whether it would be another century before the Cubs won the World Series again.

It was excruciating to sit through the rest of the meal I didn't taste when all I wanted to do was text Jay and tell him it was a go. But I bided my time and Liam couldn't tell I wasn't 100% mentally there with him.

We finally cleared our plates and Liam insisted he do the dishes since I cooked. I thanked him, kissed his cheek, and escaped to our bedroom, my cell phone in hand. *It's a go!* I texted Jay.

I had to wait three agonizing minutes to hear back. *Fantastic!*

*How are things going with Sherry?*

*She's in, too. I got the thumbs up from her this evening.*

I wanted to scream in excitement. After all this time and all our planning, this was going to happen. *How does it work now?*

*I'll call the club tomorrow and arrange everything. I'll get back to you tomorrow.*

*I'll be eagerly waiting to hear from you. I can't believe we are going to do this!*

*Hang tough, baby. It's not long from now until I fuck you until you can't walk.*

Ding, ding, ding! I loved his dirty talk. *Can't wait, Jay!*

*Me neither, baby. I'll text you tomorrow with the details.*

I dropped my phone on the nightstand and lay back on the bed. I closed my eyes and flung an arm over my face to block the light that was knocking at my eyelids. I couldn't stop thinking about my night ahead with Jay. I had no idea what a swinging club entailed but it didn't matter as I'd be sequestered away with Jay, hopefully.

I felt rather than heard Liam enter the bedroom. I kept my eyes closed, pretending to be dozing. I wanted to sit with my thoughts of Jay and not chitchat about inconsequential stuff.

Liam was rustling through the closet as I mused about the type of outfit I would buy for the swinging night. Fancy lingerie was a given. I thought my legs were my best feature so a short hemline and a garter belt with stockings were a must. A dress or skirt would both work. I'd decide which one to go with once I was at the store.

Something covered the top half of my face and I jumped, startled by the unexpected sensation. But I was immediately pushed back to the bed by a pair of strong hands on my shoulders. "What the…," I started to say but a hand clamped over my mouth.

"Shh," Liam whispered; I knew it was him by the tone of his voice.

What was going on? Liam was the most straight-laced, predictable guy in the bedroom. While I was always left satisfied, creativity wasn't typically part of our sexual routine. The most outrageous thing we'd done was watch a porn movie together one night when we'd both had too much to drink and then had sex like the actors on the screen - doggie style over the arm of the couch. That wasn't going to land us on David Letterman's Top Ten List of Sexual Adventurers.

"Lift your head an inch," Liam said in his quiet voice.

I did and felt the material that covered my eyes tighten. "Wha…," I tried again but a hand cut me off.

"Shh." The hand left my mouth and traveled down my neck, over my collarbone, and down my arm to my wrist. Something was wrapped around it and my arm was raised above my head. Our headboard was made of wooden spindles and my wrist was tied to one of the rods.

When Liam's hand took a hold of my other wrist, I pulled it free of his grip. "Why are you…"

"Hush," Liam cut me off. "Stop talking or I'll shove a sock in your mouth."

Whoa - where had this aggressive, sexual beast come from? If I hadn't heard his voice, I would've thought someone other than my husband was in the room with me. I loved the assertiveness and the stream of wetness that flooded my core was proof of that.

Liam took my wrist in his hand again, this time roughly. He yanked my arm above my head and tied my wrist next to the first one. Other than the ability to flail my legs, I was immobile.

Liam moved off the bed. I heard more rustling before his weight settled back onto the mattress. He wrapped his hand slowly around my ankle. He held it there while I fought the urge to move. I took deep, cleansing breaths to calm myself. This was so out of the ordinary that I had an odd urge to panic.

Once I'd chilled out a bit, Liam moved his hand up my leg. As slow as a snail. Inch by glorious inch. By the time he arrived at my upper thigh, my body was turning to mush as my horniness meter ramped up. When his fingers were an inch from my panty line, he took his hand off me. "Don't stop," I begged; my clit was aching to be touched.

Liam's leap off the bed was immediate. He was back seconds later, forcing my mouth open by shoving a strip of material between my lips. I tried to ask him to give me one more chance, to swear that I would stop talking, but my words were already garbled from the material in my mouth.

"Head up," Liam ordered and I lifted my neck off the pillow. He tied a knot in the material at the back of my head before pushing me against the pillow. "Don't interrupt me again," he said.

Liam shifted down the bed and took my other ankle in his hand. He worked those fingers up my leg, going agonizingly slowly again. I was ready to scream by the time he reached the top of my inner thigh. Not that I could scream if I wanted to. That time he kept going, mercifully. A finger slipped under my panty line, not far from my clit. I was hit with a wave of relief, which was quickly doused when his fingers snapped the thin material back into place and kept meandering down my leg.

When his hand reached my knee, his fingers were replaced with his mouth. He nibbled on the sensitive skin on the inside of my leg by my knee and then kissed his way up the inside of my thigh. When he reached my panties, his hands pushed the bottom of my skirt up to my waist and his mouth kept going. He kissed my mound through my lacy panties as he worked his way from one side to the other. His teeth made tiny nibbles as he passed over my clit area.

When his mouth kept going, kissing its way down my other leg, I tried not to let my frustration show; doing so might make Liam go even slower and I was already panting for action. He took his time kissing a path from my crotch to the back of my left knee.

Liam must be getting as horny as I was. Hopefully he'd fuck me soon. I tried to spread my legs even wider to entice him but he had a firm grip on the leg that he was kissing. So much for that plan.

Liam gave my knee one last kiss before he moved up my body. His fingers curled around the waistband of my skirt and he pulled it down, over my hips and my thighs. Again, he went pathetically slow. Damn, this was getting to be uncomfortable. Having an orgasm sitting inside me simmering, needing to be stoked, was agonizing.

Liam pulled my skirt free of my body and I heard it land with a whoosh on the floor. He crawled up the bed, stopping when he was sitting on top of me, his legs straddling my hips. His weight felt like a blanket of bricks on top of my lower torso, a sexy and comfortable blanket. His jeans were chafing my bare skin but I didn't care. Any sensations were a turn on at that point.

I was wearing a t-shirt. Liam pulled it tight against me as he played with the bottom of it. He began rolling it up slowly, like I imagine a cigar would be rolled. He continued going up my stomach and over my chest. As he rolled my shirt over my bra, my nipples went from perky to hard as nails. Liam ignored them and kept rolling - up my neck, over my face, and up my raised arms. He left it bunched around my wrists and moved back down my body and off the bed. I felt exposed lying there, tied to the bed and wearing only my bra and panties. I also felt more aroused than I had been in years. This was so out of character for Liam, making what would come next an unknown factor. It caused my blood to race in an exhilarating way.

Liam was moving around the room. I could feel him going from one place to another and back again but as I was blindfolded, I couldn't see what he was doing of course. I stretched my legs straight out in front of me, working out some nervous energy.

Liam spoke, startling me in the otherwise silent room. "So, you want to go swinging. You want to feel something other than me inside you. I get that, I really do." I tried to tell him that that wasn't it at all but my words were muffled beyond recognition behind the gag.

Liam continued, "Well, let's not make you wait until swinging night to get fucked hard. I'll give it to you good, just like you want."

Hell yeah! My body was clamoring for action. Bring it on, Liam!

"Open your legs," he said. I opened them. "Wider," he ordered. My knees were almost touching the mattress at my sides. How much wider did he think I could go without snapping my legs off?

His hand curled into my panties. His knuckles grazed my mound as he gripped the lace. He gave it a hard tug and ripped the material off my body. Holy shit! A tsunami of wetness flooded my core. I was so ready to be fucked.

Liam gripped my thigh with one hand, holding my leg steady. After a pause, something circled around my pussy lips. I couldn't tell what it was but every time it grazed my clit, my orgasm flared a little brighter. Yes!

Something shoved its way all the way inside me. My pussy reacted instantly, squeezing and pulsing around it. The hard length stroked in and out of manically, faster than I've ever been fucked by a cock. It was vibrating as it stroked me. It must be a vibrator or dildo of some sort. I stopped questioning what was inside me and sank my head deeper into the pillow to focus on nothing but enjoying the moment.

The plundering continued nonstop. My pussy was starting to ache but it was a soreness that I welcomed. It's been years since my body felt a fucking the following day; I would still be feeling this tomorrow without a doubt.

Liam's hand on my thigh started meandering up my leg. It trailed up to my belly button and fell back down to my core. His thumb lightly touched my clit, barely enough to make its presence known. But the intensity increased and the elusive orgasm drew rapidly closer. I was so ready for it that I couldn't think of anything else.

Liam continued fucking me hard with the vibrator as he stroked my clit. As was likely his intention, I came with the power of a Mack truck barrelling down the highway. It was a big one and my whole body seized up as it was ploughed down by the force.

I climaxed for longer than I usually did, my body not having the chance to start the recovery process as Liam kept up his relentless assault.

And that continued. I desperately needed a breather, a few moments to recover from what I'd been through, but Liam didn't give it to me. His fingers played nonstop with my clit, threatening to rub it raw. And it still drove me crazy. Another orgasm flared as the current one was still peaking.

I took deep breaths, calming myself. I loved rough sex - and I haven't had it this rough in years - so I focused on revelling in every touch, every pump.

Liam's arms must've been getting sore but he kept up his intense fucking pace with the dildo. My second orgasm continued to grow closer; it was passing the first one, which was now fading away.

I erupted again, taking me by surprise with its rapid approach and attack. The second orgasm was just as powerful, bowling me over from the inside out. Liam kept stroking my clit, extending my peak as I absorbed the sexual energy that was flowing through me. Those weren't regular orgasms I'd had; they were sexual sledgehammers whacking me upside the head. And hitting me deep in my core. I made sure I was always sexually satisfied when I had sex but this took it to a whole new level.

When I was well on my way to recovering from orgasm #2, Liam pulled the dildo out of me and took his hand out of my crotch. His weight shifted off the bed and I figured that was it. I wasn't sure how much more my body, especially my pussy, could take.

I was wrong - Liam was nowhere near finished. "My turn," he said as he moved back onto the mattress. "I hope you liked the pussy pounding. I'm guessing that's what you are aiming for with the swing…"

It was futile for Liam to ask me questions since I couldn't answer him. But I think Liam liked it that way.

I flinched as warm liquid hit my chest. I thought for a second that Liam had peed on me but the smell of vanilla that tickled my nostrils let me know I was wrong.

Liam rubbed his hands over the oily fluid, tweaking my nipples as he passed over them. He was balancing the line perfectly between pleasure and pain.

As he continued rubbing my chest, Liam settled above me, his legs resting on either side of my ribs. Another squirt of fluid hit me and Liam rubbed that over my already slick chest.

I was wondering what the point was of the titty slip and slide when Liam squeezed my tits together and shoved his dick between them. He rubbed himself back and forth in the valley between my boobs, his hands holding my tits in a vice-like grip.

"Oh yeah. I've always wanted to fuck your tits. You have great tits."

I didn't even bother to moan a response as it was pointless.

The titty fucking continued. Liam would stop every so often to spank my nipples with his cock. I'd never been tit fucked before. It wasn't doing much for me but Liam was obviously enjoying it, judging by his moans and groans.

He abruptly pulled back from me and moved back to the end of the bed. He clenched my hips and flipped me over, as easily if I'd been a pancake in a frying pan. My arms were crossed above my head and my boobs were mashed into the mattress.

Liam ran his hands roughly up the back of my thighs and onto my ass. He squeezed my butt cheeks hard, digging his nails into my flesh. I cried out, as much as someone gagged and restrained could cry out. He was crossing the line from pleasure into unbearable pain but just before it became too much, he let go of my ass.

He took a hold of my hips and lifted my ass high into the air. One hand rubbed my ass while his other spanked my butt with his cock. His ramrod hard cock that I was more than ready for him to drive into me.

As he continued to spank me, Liam rambled, "I'm guessing this is what you want. Rough, anonymous sex with a faceless guy at the swinging club. I'm happy to oblige you now. I'm gonna fuck you until you can't see straight. Just pretend we're swinging now and get off on that."

While his words could've sounded harsh to some people, they were nothing but a turn on to me. Liam was still rambling on, "... and don't think I won't enjoy every minute of fucking another tight, hot pussy. I love yours - you are always so wet and tight - but I am going to pound the shit out of someone else. I might even make her…"

Liam drove into me, cutting off the rest of his sentence. Clutching at my hips like he was trying to fuse my hipbones with his palms, he fucked me like I'd never been fucked from behind before.

Relentlessly and unmercifully, he drove me forward with each thrust. My body didn't stop until my skull was pinned against the headboard. My hands gripped the bars above my head, trying to hold myself as steady as I could considering Liam's cock was impaling me relentlessly.

Liam let go of me with one hand and slid that hand into my core. He continued his fucking pace as his fingers rubbed my clit. My nub was already swollen and tender so I thought I couldn't handle anymore. I was wrong. A dozen strokes later, I knew a third orgasm was a possibility.

Liam kept everything at a manic pace - his clit rubbing and his pussy fucking. I ignored the kink in my neck and soaked it all in. Relaxing into the pummelling spurred my orgasm on even faster.

I'd lost all sense of time. I was living in touches and sensations, not seconds or minutes. And orgasms. The third one hit and obliterated the after-effects of the first and second ones. I came with such intensity that I blacked out for a moment. But only a moment as Liam slapped my ass hard, bringing me back. My body had relaxed and was sliding down toward the bed when Liam gripped my hips again, yanking me up. "Oh yeah, squeeze me," he yelled in a gruff tone I'd never heard before. It dawned on me that my core was spasming violently from my orgasm, likely trying to squeeze the life out of Liam's cock.

I was still cresting the climax when Liam pulled out of me and screamed, "Hell yeah!" Droplets of cum shot all over my back like liquid bullets from an assault rifle. The spray hadn't even started to lessen when Liam shoved his shaft back into me, my tender pussy embracing him yet again. He slowly did a few lengths in and out of my body before he pumped hard into me one last time and collapsed onto my back.

With my neck still at an awkward angle against the headboard, my bound hands numb, and a human blanket on top of me, logic would think I would be uncomfortable. But I wasn't; the opposite was true. The orgasms had been so earth shattering that all I was left with was a deep, satisfying soul-reaching exhaustion.

I was dozing off when Liam rolled off me. Lying next to me, he took off my gag and untied my wrists from the headboard. He rubbed my hands and wrists gently until the blood flow returned.

Liam pulled me into the crook of his arm and I rested my head on his chest. The arm that wasn't pinned underneath me I flung over his torso. Liam's free hand reached over to stroke my arm. "How was that for you?" he asked. "Is that what you are looking for in a swing?"

Talk about landmine questions. I had to tread carefully. "I loved every moment of that," I replied. "I love when you are a beast."

Liam repeated the question I'd left unanswered. "That the kind of thing you are hoping to get from swinging?"

I really didn't want to answer that but like a dog with a bone, Liam wasn't going to let it go. "It's more of a curiosity thing. The stories Janice told were interesting."

Liam grunted in response but I didn't say anything else; my desperation to avoid that conversation was closing in on panic level. It would be devastating if Liam decided that he was no longer willing to go to the swinging club.

"You hungry?" I asked.

"Surprisingly yes."

I rolled out of Liam's arms and off the bed. As I slid my clothes back on, I asked, "Shall I make us some nachos or a bowl of pasta?"

"Let's do nachos."

"Okay. You relax and I'll get them started."

The rest of the evening flew by as we fell back into our regular night-time routine, the only difference was my body still tingling from Liam's pummellings.

On my way to work the next day, I texted Jay. *Any updates? I'm so excited that I'm impatient.*

Jay didn't leave me hanging for long. *How does not this Saturday but the following Saturday work for you guys?*

*That should be fine.*

*Okay. I'll book all four of us in at The Swinger's Club. 9 p.m.*

*THANK YOU!!* If I hadn't been sitting in my car, I would've jumped up and down screaming in excitement.

*No need to thank me.* Another text from Jay followed 30 seconds later. *That's not true. You can thank me by sucking my dick in two Saturdays.*

*Deal! I can't wait!*

*Me neither. What is your hubby's type so I can do my best to make sure Sherry will appeal to him?*

I thought about that for a moment. I knew Liam was attracted to me - he'd proved that thousands of times - but I wasn't what usually floated his boat, if we were speaking physically. *He likes redheads with big boobs. And he's a leg man.*

*Okay. I'll make it happen.*

*Jay, thanks for arranging all of this. I can't wait to see you.*

*Me neither, baby. I can't wait to touch you again.*

*I'm with you on that.*

*I'm heading into a meeting. I'll be in touch.*

*Ok. Have a great day.*

*You 2. Xoxox*

The Xs and Os warmed the darkest reaches of my heart. I put my phone into my purse, stepped out of my car, and made myself go into the building to work. I didn't want to be there, I wanted to be at home with my thoughts of the thrilling night approaching us.

#####

My palms were sweating when I brought up the swing with Liam that night. "How does two Saturdays from now work for you?"

"For what?"

"To give The Swinger's Club a try."

Liam pulled out his phone and scrolled, I'm guessing to check his calendar. "That whole day is free for me."

"Good. Because we're booked in for that evening at nine. We could've changed, of course, if you'd had something already planned for that night."

"Nope. I'm all clear." Liam was tapping away on his phone. "The 20th, right?" he asked.

"Yes."

"All set," he said, putting his phone down.

"Okay."

With that, the swinging night was cemented in place. It was going to be a long ten days waiting for the 20th to arrive but we were so close now, relatively speaking.

#####

"You ready?" Liam asked.

I'd been inspecting my outfit in the mirror and I caught Liam's eye over my shoulder. I threw him a smile, trying to settle my nerves. "I think I'm ready." I'd changed my mind a dozen times as to what to wear and had finally settled on a short but classy skirt and a sleeveless button-down blouse. I'd thrown a wrap around my shoulders in case the club was chilly. I slid into my highest heels, adding a few inches to my 5'7" height.

"You look beautiful," Liam said, coming up behind me and taking a hold of my shoulders. As he planted a kiss on my neck, I breathed in a deep whiff of his cologne. A wave of love rushed through me that my husband cared enough to give us the gift of this night. He didn't know the back-story behind it, of course, which was for the best.

As Liam let go of me, I said, "You look very spiffy yourself. I've always loved that suit on you." He was wearing a black number that made his fit and trim body look even more lean and strong. Tonight he'd paired it with a plain white shirt and a red tie. He looked every inch the successful man he was.

We locked up the house and drove eastward toward the club. Without the exact address, it would've been tough to find as the name wasn't blazoned across the building. Instead, the address was simply displayed above an unmarked door with three letters in gold underneath - TSC.

We stepped inside the building and I was hit with a wave of relief. All the planning Jay and I had done and all the subtle manipulations of Liam and Sherry had paid off. We were here!

Liam and I checked in at the reservation desk and proceeded into the club. I stopped inside the door, my mouth no doubt gaping open. The club was massive. It looked like it was a converted warehouse that covered an entire city block. The space was open from one end to the other with a second floor covering half the space above us, the other half left open like a gigantic loft area. The ceiling must've been 30 feet high at least, making the space feel even larger than it already was.

"Wow," Liam whispered as he stood beside me, each of his eyes as big as a yoyo.

"Yeah," I seconded. It was a lot to take in, akin to driving down the Las Vegas strip for the first time.

"Shall we grab a drink?" Liam asked.

"Sure," I replied. Getting a drink would give us a chance to catch our breath. And I could keep an eye out for Jay.

One continuous bar circled three sides of the club. We found two empty stools and sat down. Liam ordered a Heineken. I opted for a cranberry juice and club soda so I could keep my thoughts straight. After we'd come so far, Jay and I, I didn't want everything to fall apart because I was tipsy and did something to screw up our chance to be together.

Neither of us spoke as we sipped our drinks and looked around. The place was packed. Who would have thought there were so many swingers in Chicago?

I was starting to worry that it would be impossible to find Jay and Sherry. And I had no interest in having sex with anyone else despite the number of very attractive men in the room.

"Where's the nearest ladies room?" I asked the closest bartender.

"Go to the end of this row and take a right."

"Thanks." I turned to Liam. "Don't go anywhere or I'll never find you. I'll be right back."

"Okay."

Once I was locked in a bathroom stall, I pulled my phone from my purse and texted Jay. *Where are you? I don't want us to miss each other tonight.*

I waited a couple of minutes but Jay didn't respond. I could see that my text to him had been delivered but hadn't been read. I sent him another text. *I'm at the bar close to the entrance on the right side. Please come find us!*

I shoved my phone back in my purse, made a pretence of washing my hands, and meandered back to where Liam was still sitting, keeping my eyes out for Jay the entire time. No luck.

Liam was chatting with a cute blonde who'd taken up residence on my seat. On her other side was a hot, nerdy guy who looked bored to be there. I sidled up beside my husband and put my arm around his shoulders. "Hey," I said, interrupting their conversation.

Liam put an arm around my waist. "Tiffany, I'd like you to meet Jessica," he said. "Jessica, this is my wife, Tiffany." We shook hands as a trickle of panic raced through me. What if

Liam found a couple he was determined to hook up with before we connected with Jay and Sherry?

"Nice to meet you, Tiffany," the perky blonde said. "This is my husband, Howard," she said, indicating the nerd to her right.

Howard grunted but didn't look our way. Jessica shrugged his rude behavior off and returned to chatting with Liam. I tuned them out as I scanned the room, desperate to spot Jay. I was tempted to pull my phone from my purse to see if Jay had replied but that would be too obvious.

"What do you say, Tiffany?" Liam asked, drawing me back to their conversation.

"What?"

"Shall we go to a private room with Jessica and Howard?"

Oh, fuck! I had to nip this in the bud right now. Even if Jay weren't a factor in tonight's equation, I wouldn't let Howard touch me with a ten-foot long pole.

I turned to Jessica, a fake but hopefully convincing expression of regret on my face. "I'd normally love to. But this is our first time at this swinging thing. I'd like a little time to wander around and get a feel for the place. Soak it all in. Maybe we'll run into you later." I would do what I could to make sure that didn't happen.

Jessica looked disappointed but she was smart enough to recognize a brush off when she heard one. I grabbed Liam's hand and pulled him away from the bar before anyone could argue with what I'd said.

"What was up with that?" Liam asked.

"Howard creeped me out. No way was I going to do anything with him. We can find a couple that we both like."

"Okay," Liam conceded. I could tell that he wasn't happy to leave Jessica but he'd seen Howard's disinterest so he probably understood where I was coming from.

"Shall we go upstairs and see what is going on up there?"

"Sure."

We meandered around until we found a staircase. Once on the second floor, we had a much better view of the entire space. We took a seat at a row of benches along the railing while my eyes searched for Jay.

"What's up with the rooms?" Liam asked.

"Huh?" My one-track mind was having trouble focusing on anything other than keeping an eye out for Jay.

"The rooms behind us - what do you make of them?"

I forced myself to look around at what Liam was talking about. Dozens of small room with signs on their doors that could be flipped to either 'vacant' or 'occupied' circled the entire top floor. "I'm guessing they are for when people want to get down to business. No one is going at it in the main area," I pointed out.

"True. Nice to have privacy." Liam had never been an exhibitionist so he would need a room with a door in order to get in the mood.

"Excuse me," someone behind us said. It was a voice from the past. I rapidly stood and took in the sight of Jay and a gorgeous redhead that I assumed was Sherry. I felt a smile of relief and joy cross my face but I quickly reined it in. As far as Liam knew, these two were strangers to both of us. It took every iota of willpower not to throw my arms around Jay.

Liam spoke up. "Hello," he said, his eyes locked on Sherry's ample cleavage.

"Can we join you?" Jay asked.

"Sure, sure. Please," Liam replied, indicating the empty space on the bench. Sherry sat next to Liam and they immediately dove into conversation. Jay sat next to Sherry and I plunked down next to him. Our thighs were touching and it was excruciating to not be able to touch more of him. Soon enough, I knew I would.

Sherry had her back to Jay as she chatted with Liam so I took the opportunity to clutch at Jay's knee. "Thank God," I mouthed and Jay smiled at me.

I think he could tell I was in a bit of shock as he carried on a surface conversation with me while I pulled myself together. I couldn't stop staring at him. I'd seen dozens of pictures of him on Facebook but he looked so much better in person. He was dressed in black pressed jeans and a black long-sleeved buttonless shirt that fit him like a second skin. It was obvious he took care of himself. I couldn't wait to get him undressed and inside me.

I watched Jay's lips move but his words weren't registering. I really needed to pull myself together and focus on what was happening. It was tough as I had been transported back to when we'd almost become lovers in my Ford Festiva. We were finally going to finish what we started!

Jay put his hand on my arm and I jumped; electricity was coursing through my veins. I was stunned how a light touch could send me to the sexual moon. I couldn't begin to imagine what would happen when Jay was making love to me. "Tiffany, you gotta pull it together. Baby, focus," Jay whispered.

I shook my head as if I could shake the fog off my brain. "What?" I answered.

"Sherry and Liam are going to get suspicious. Try and act like we just met."

I nodded and took a few deep breaths. *Here and now, here and now* I chanted silently to myself. It was next to impossible when I was drowning in Jay's blue eyes, their depths seeming to never end. Two more deep breaths. Okay, I've got this.

Sherry abruptly turned and poked her head in our direction. She looked at Jay and raised her eyebrows. "Sure," he said to her.

Sherry looked at me. "You cool if I take Liam to a private room?" she asked.

I almost fainted with relief but managed to nod. The duo stood and Liam looked at me. "You okay with this?" he asked.

I threw him a thumbs up sign as I knew I was incapable of speaking.

I watched them wander away and duck into a room with a 'vacant' sign, flipping it over before they closed the door.

I turned to Jay, able to finally focus on him without censorship. I climbed onto his lap facing him, a thigh on each side of his hips. I threw my arms around his shoulders and hugged him so tight that no one would've been able to slide a hand between our bodies. Jay hugged me back just as tight, one of his arms snaking around my waist, the other underneath my butt to hold me upright against him in case I'd been struck by the stupid stick and released my grip.

We sat there in silence, clinging to each other, as I composed myself. When I could speak again, I whispered in his ear, "It is so good to see you, Jay. I never fully believed this moment would ever come."

"Nothing would keep me from your forever, baby."

"I'm so glad."

"Hey, shall we get a room for ourselves?"

I pulled back from Jay so I could look at his face. "That is the best idea I've heard since you got out of my car."

The way Jay grinned at me made it clear that he knew I was referring to the moment we'd almost been lovers back when we were 18.

I uncurled myself off Jay's lap with as much finesse as I could muster, working hard not to give anyone a panty peep show. Jay took my hand and we walked the opposite direction from where Liam and Sherry had gone. "How's this?" he asked when we reached a vacant room.

Without looking at the space, I answered, "Perfect - anywhere you are is where I want to be." I was so overjoyed to see Jay that the cheesy words were flowing out of my mouth.

Jay gestured for me to enter the room and I did, watching him flip the sign and close the door behind him.

Silence surrounded us, as well as a crackle of electricity. You could touch the sexual tension in the room as Jay and I looked at one another, neither of us speaking. He grinned at me, that sexy, mischievous smile that made it clear that we were about to have some heavy-duty fun.

I backed into a corner, my body coiled with sexual anticipation. My crotch was growing more wet with every passing second. Jay approached me slowly, never taking his eyes off me. I could feel my nipples tighten as my mind processed thoughts of what was going to happen.

When Jay was within arm's reach, I raised a hand to touch him. Before my hand could connect, he grabbed my wrist and dropped my arm by my side. "Just let me touch you for a few minutes."

It wasn't a question but I nodded in response anyway and mentally cemented my arms to my sides.

With only a fingertip, he touched the side of my face. He trailed the finger down my neck and onto the bare skin above the 'V' of my blouse neckline. He undid the buttons on my shirt, one at a time with the speed of a sloth. The anticipation was agony but I knew it would make our lovemaking even better because of it.

My blouse fell open as Jay undid the last button. He slid it off my shoulders and dropped it onto the closest chair. His eyes took in my boobs that were framed by a black bra that had cost me a fortune; judging by Jay's stunned face and open mouth, it was worth every penny.

He cupped my boobs, his fingers caressing my nipples through the lacy material. I watched Jay's eyes grow even bigger as my nipples grew as hard as stones under his touch.

I was aching to feel his hands on me without the bra between his skin and mine. I unglued my arms from my sides to reach behind my back. Jay moved his hands from my chest and grabbed both my wrists, pulling them down again. "I want you to touch my naked tits," I said.

Jay's eyes grew dark. He let go of my wrists and slithered his hands around my body to cup my back. He walked his fingers down to my bra strap and took his time working the clasp undone.

As the material fell loose on my body, my boobs shivered with a wave of relief from being freed from their lacy prison. Jay slid his fingers around the straps on my shoulders and slid them down and off my arms. The bra followed where my blouse had gone, landing in the growing pile on the chair.

Cupping my boobs on their undersides, Jay looked at my tits like he was staring at the Holy Grail. "I've dreamed of seeing these for years," Jay said. "They're even more spectacular than I thought they would be."

What do you say to that? Thank you was inadequate so I opted to say nothing. I closed my eyes and rested my head on the wall behind me as Jay made love to my tits. Every inch of them was licked and sucked. My nipples grew harder than they ever had before. Jay's touch ignited every part of my body, just by mauling my tits.

I was about to melt into the wall behind me when Jay pulled his face free of my chest and stood up straight. His mouth was inches from mine. I thought he was going to kiss me but I was wrong; he used his mouth to share a fantasy. "You know, ever since I last saw you, I've wanted to make love to you. I've wanted that more with each passing day. I dreamt of being inside you every day. A thousand times as I fucked Sherry, I imagined it was you that I was pounding into. As crazy as that is, there is one thing I've wanted to do even more than screw you."

"What's that?" I asked, half excited, half fearful for what the answer would be.

"I've wanted to watch your face as you get off from me touching you. That I have fantasized about even more than fucking you."

Damn! Jay knew exactly what to say drive me crazy with lust. What woman wouldn't want to know that she had been that adored, that desired? I couldn't think of one.

I was so overwhelmed that I couldn't speak. Looking at Jay, I nodded, giving him the go-ahead to do whatever he wanted.

I leaned back against the wall, my arms still hanging at my sides, as I gave my body over to Jay to do with as he pleased. His hands slid from my tits to the waistband of my skirt. He found the zipper on the side and slowly inched it down. When it couldn't go any further, he gently pushed the material down my hips, the skirt eventually pooling at my feet. I lifted one foot and moved it to the outside of the skirt puddle. My other foot dug under the material with the toe of my stiletto and kicked it away from us so my feet wouldn't get tangled in it.

That left me standing in only my panties, a black thong that matched the bra that had been tossed aside. Jay let out a whistle as his eyes devoured the sight of me standing in front of him, naked except for a patch of material covering my pussy. "Damn, baby, you look good enough to eat. But that'll come later…"

I had no doubt that it would. And I couldn't wait. But first things first.

Jay ran his hands down my hips, his fingers twisting in the strings on the sides of my thong. "I just don't know," he mumbled to himself. He looked slightly overwhelmed so I opted to say nothing.

Jay ripped at both sides of my thong, startling me as I didn't see that move coming. A moan escaped from my mouth before I realised it was there. "Did you like that?" Jay asked.

"Apparently." If the wetness pooling in my core was any indication, I loved it.

Jay's hand slid between my legs and I leaned back again, needing the wall to hold me up against the barrage of sensations. His fingers wasted no time, immediately alternating between stroking my clit and sinking into my depths. When his fingers were inside me, he rubbed my pussy walls, occasionally hitting my G-spot. My legs threatened to give out each time he hit my sweet spot but I managed to remain standing.

His other hand moved up to my shoulder. Two fingers and a thumb circled around the bottom of my neck while the other two fingers dug into my shoulder. The pressure sent erotic chills down to my thighs. His lips kissed random parts of my body - my neck, my collarbone, my cheek, a nipple - but all I could focus on was what was happening in my crotch.

I didn't want to cum yet but I couldn't stop myself. The days and years of build up to that moment combined with what Jay was doing to my pussy caused me to lose all control. I screamed Jay's name as I came, my entire body tensing and then spasming as the full power of my orgasm hit me. Jay kept touching my insides, my pussy walls tightening around his fingers; I couldn't wait until it was his cock inside me. Hopefully that would happen next.

Jay said something but my shattered mind couldn't register the words. "What's that?" I mumbled.

"Do you like the taste of yourself?"

I couldn't figure out what he meant. "What?" I asked, my brain not ready for more than simple thoughts.

Jay spoke slower, clueing in that I wasn't with it yet. "Do you like the taste of your own pussy?"

Did I? I wasn't sure so I shrugged.

"Open up," he said.

Open what? I couldn't open my core up any further than it already was. Before I could ask him for clarification, Jay said, "Open your mouth."

I parted my lips and Jay slid his fingers inside. Tartness hit my tongue first, followed by a touch of sweet that caused my taste buds to burst to life. I closed my lips around his fingers and sucked myself off him. Not bad. I could see why some men loved pussy juice.

Jay pulled his hand free of my face and asked, "Want to sit down?" He gestured toward the bed.

"I'm good." I was still leaning against the wall but my strength was rapidly coming back. "What I want is to not be the only naked person in this room." Below Jay's neck, the only skin I could see was his hands. And judging by the outline of the hard-on through Jay's pants, I doubted I was the only one who wanted him naked.

"Can we do one thing first?" Jay didn't wait for me to answer. He took my arm and led me to the bed, abruptly pushing me onto it.

I flailed back, my arms flung out to my sides, my hair fanning onto the pillow above my head. My legs were hanging off the bed from my knees down, my toes close to touching the floor. Jay stood at the end of the bed, towering over me. My nipples tightened as he looked at my naked body as if I was a smorgasbord and he was starving.

Jay reached into his back pocket and took out his phone, giving it his 100% attention. Really? He was choosing this moment to check his e-mail? Or to answer some texts? A flash of anger hit me. I went to roll off the bed but Jay grabbed my thigh. "Where are you going?" he asked.

"To give you some privacy with your phone." I sounded petty, I was sure, but I didn't care.

He ignored my words. "I need you to watch something," he said, passing his phone to me. A video started playing and I felt like a dolt. Jay moved a pillow under my head while I focused on the image on the screen. It was Jay in what looked like a bedroom. I turned the volume up on the phone as Jay started speaking on the screen. "Hey, baby. I can't believe I'm seeing you in a few short hours. I am so excited and I want to show you how much."

He'd been wearing a robe, which he took off and dropped on the bed behind him. He was naked and his body was spectacular, his muscles barely contained by his skin. I wanted to lick the screen.

On camera, Jay spent a few seconds fussing with his phone, propping it onto a dresser or shelf. When he was done and stepped away from the camera, I could see his entire body above his knees. Holy shit! I almost came again just looking at him. His cock was hard and pointing at me. Oh yeah! I wanted him so bad. I wanted that cock inside me, fucking me hard.

I looked up at Jay. He was still standing at the end of the bed. He was looking at me with a naughty expression. "Keep watching," he said.

I turned my attention back to the screen where Jay was slowly stroking himself. He spoke again, "I can't wait to be inside you. But before I fuck you, I want to eat your pussy. So lay back, relax, and watch me eat you out. Well, only if you want to. I'm cool if you just want to shut your eyes and enjoy my mouth in your pussy."

Jay grabbed my ankles and pulled me to the end of the bed, stopping when my butt hung over the end. He pushed my legs apart and his face dove to my core as I continued to watch Jay play with himself in the video.

Jay's tongue was fucking me as he spoke on the screen, his hand not slowing down on his cock. "I can just imagine it now. You are watching this as I chow down on you. I've thought nonstop about how you will taste. I bet you'll be sweet with a touch of fruitiness. Whatever you taste like, I know I'll love it as it's you." He picked up his self-stroking speed as he continued talking, "Soon after that, I'll have my hard dick, this hard dick, in your pussy. Now that is a whole other matter. I've imagined how tight and wet you'd be every single day since I last saw you. You'll squeeze my dick so hard I'll have to work to keep from cuming as soon as I slide inside you. But I'll do whatever it takes to hold off."

I gasped, startling myself as Jay's tongue moved from fucking my pussy hole to flicking my clit. I paused the video and closed my eyes as my body fought to deal with the sensations racing through me. My first orgasm hadn't totally died out and it flared up again, rapidly morphing into the beginnings of orgasm #2. If he kept up the tongue-on-clit action, I'd erupt into his mouth before long.

Just when I thought I had my body under control, Jay slid a finger inside me, his tongue not missing a stroke. His tongue had been overwhelming enough but adding a finger to the mix ramped my body up even more.

Needing to get my focus off what was going on between my legs, I unpaused the video and continued watching it. On the screen, Jay had stopped talking for the moment. His eyes were shut as he continued stroking his cock. Seeing his hard shaft made my body physically ache.

I wasn't beneath begging, "Jay, as much as I love you eating me out, I want you to fuck me. Can you please do that?"

He pulled his face out of my core to answer me. "Oh, I can, of course, but not quite yet, baby. Hang tough." His tongue returned to my clit with a renewed vigour.

It had been worth a shot. My eyes shifted back to the video. I was getting even hornier watching Jay play with himself. And orgasm #2 continued to draw steadily closer.

The Jay on the screen started talking again. "Hot damn, Tiff. Just thinking of you tonight has me ready to blow. I want you to watch me shoot. I'm going to pretend I'm cuming all over your tits. Speaking of your tits, I can't wait to see them. I have no doubt they will be amazing. I plan to gnaw on your nipples until you beg me to stop. Oh yeah, baby. Then I'm gonna fuck you until we both explode. Speaking of exploding, watch closely."

My eyes moved from his face to his delicious cock. Jay stroked himself even faster than he had been before coming to a stop, angling the head of his cock toward the camera. A big wad of jism shot out, arcing toward the screen before falling short. A couple more streams of cum burst out of him before falling out of the camera view.

Watching Jay was such a turn on that I couldn't stop the orgasm that hit me like a sledge hammer, the epicenter bombarding my pussy area before spreading through the rest of my body.

My arms fell to my sides, Jay's phone slipping out of my hand. Through my orgasm-induced brain fog, I heard the gadget hit the floor. But I couldn't move to get it. Jay was still tweaking my clit with his tongue, drawing out the tendrils of the orgasm.

I lay back, taking every delicious sensation in. The second orgasm had been even more powerful than the first, the waves of pleasure doubly explosive. The peak lasted longer, too, drilling deep into my core.

Minutes later, I opened my eyes. Jay was still kneeling on the floor at the end of the bed. He had a hand on the top of each of my thighs and was looking at me with the goofiest grin. "You are the most beautiful creature," he said.

I'm sure I blushed but Jay probably didn't notice as my entire body was still flushed. When I opted not to answer, he said, "I'll never forget the look on your face when you cum."

Eager to change the subject, I said, "Enough about me. How about we finally get your clothes off? I want to ravage you."

Fire burst in Jay's eyes; I could tell my words turned him on. I sat up and reached for him, determined to pull his shirt over his head and off. But he stepped back out of my reach. "C'mon," I begged, ready for cock action.

"I want that, too. Trust me," he said, pointing toward his very obvious hard-on in his jeans.

"Bear with me for one more thing and then I'll fuck you until you are begging me to stop as you can't take it anymore."

I tried not to let my sigh of frustration be too obvious. "Okay," I conceded.

"Can you put your skirt and top back on?" When he saw what must've been an unhappy grimace on my face, he added, "Please."

I nodded, unable to deny Jay anything that he wanted. He picked up my top and held the shoulders open so I could slip my arms through the holes. He did the same with the skirt, holding the waist apart so I could slide my legs into it. He kissed my lips as he brought the material to the top of my thighs, his hands lingering on my ass cheeks. He had the patience of a saint to be able to put off cock action a moment longer.

We left the room and headed for the stairs. The place had doubled in people since Jay and I had sequestered ourselves in our room. Holding my hand so tight that I felt the blood flow slow, Jay led me through the crowd and out the front door. "Where are we going?" I asked Jay.

"Thirty seconds, baby. Hang tough."

We rounded the end of the building and Jay pulled me toward the parking lot. As we reached the back corner, I burst out laughing as my heart overflowed. A blue Ford Festiva was tucked into a stall, beckoning to us.

I looked at Jay and gushed, "I love it!"

He dropped my hand and reached into a pocket at the front of his jeans. He pulled out a key and stuck it in the key slot to unlock it. Once the door was open, Jay pulled me to him, pinning me between his hard body and the rear door of the car. His mouth dove into my neck and his hands moved over every part of my body they could reach, igniting my skin everywhere he touched it. As he nibbled, he said, "I've fantasized about having sex with you in this car every day since I last saw you. That's a long damn time."

I wrapped my arms around his shoulders and moved them slowly down his back to his ass, pulling him tight against me. His cock ground into my pelvic bone, driving me wild. "Well, let's not wait a moment longer," I said.

Jay moved his hand between our bodies to undo his pants. I pushed his hand aside. "Let me," I said.

I made quick work of the belt buckle, button, and zipper. Finally! I slid a hand into his pants and grabbed his cock, squeezing it tight. Jay's moan was loud and guttural, music to my horny body.

A beast took possession of Jay. Pushing me back an inch, he yanked his pants down as he fell into the front passenger seat. He moved so fast I barely had a second to get a decent look at his impressive cock; all I saw was that it was hard and pointing up toward the sky. His butt planted in the seat, he leaned up and grabbed a hold of my hips, pulling me into the car. He'd somehow managed to manoeuvre me so my right knee was wedged between the seat and the gearshift. My left knee rested against the outside of his thigh. My naked core was hovering just over his shaft. With one slight move, Jay would finally be inside me. He must've had the same thought as he gripped my hips in his hands to shift me slightly to the left. The head of his cock slid in, but just the head. "Look at me," Jay ordered, his voice a few octaves lower than usual.

I'd been looking at where our bodies were about to join. I ripped my eyes from the sight of where his cock disappeared into me and looked at Jay. My hands moved to cup his jaw as I stared into his eyes. "Don't blink," he said.

I kept my eyes zoned on his as he slid the rest of the way into me, my body stretching to accommodate his girth. He smiled at me, a mischievous grin that took me back to my teen years. I couldn't resist leaning into him and gluing my lips to his, my tongue darting into his mouth. My tongue invaded him the same way his cock had invaded me - fully and with gusto.

I moved my arms around Jay's shoulders as his hands dropped to my stomach. His fingers circled my waist and squeezed tight. He pulled upward, lifting my body a couple inches up his cock. When he loosened his grip, I slid back down his length. My mouth continued to devour his as I took Jay's hint and rode him. I went slowly at first, focusing on moving from the base of his shaft to the top of his cock's head, careful that he didn't pop out of my pussy. Jay's hands slid down to cup my ass. His nails dug into the fleshy part of my butt cheeks. He pierced the skin with one of his fingernails, the pain hitting my system with an adrenaline rush.

I pulled my lips free of Jay's as I gulped in deep breaths and let out a groan that sounded like an animal in heat; I would never have thought that I was capable of making such a horrific sound. But Jay didn't seem to mind, judging by the way his eyes narrowed.

I continued riding Jay, with an animalistic urge that was more about frenzy than accuracy. Jay got into it, thrusting his hips to drive deeper into me each time I sank onto his shaft. A couple of times I bonked my head on the roof of the car but I barely noticed.

An orgasm hit me without warning. I peaked as Jay's cock skimmed my clit. My gasp sounded like a bullhorn in the tiny space, threatening to deafen both of us. My body seized up. My limbs felt like they'd been shot with liquid nitrogen. Even with Jay's hands trying to lift my hips, I couldn't move. I knew that until I finished peaking, I'd be useless.

Jay must've known that, too. Wrapping his arms around my waist, he barrel-rolled us so I was lying on the seat and he was on top of me. Reaching behind him, Jay grabbed a hold of my calves and hoisted my feet onto the dashboard. The feel of the cool glass against my toes cut through my brain fog, the first thing to register since I'd cum so abruptly.

Jay gave me no time to recover. Once he was perfectly positioned between my spread-wide legs, he drove his cock back into me, fucking me with a speed and accuracy that would've impressed the most experienced of lovers.

I reached up to run my hands along the width of Jay's shoulders, my fingertips tracing the taut muscles under his skin. My fingers kept meandering, running down his arms to where his hands gripped the headrest behind me.

I moved my hands to lightly cup his jaw, taking in the sight of his glazed eyes as he looked down at me. A bead of sweat rolled from his brow and down his cheek. I brushed it aside with my finger, my eyes mesmerized by the trail of wetness that remained on his skin.

Jay picked up his already rapid pace. He hoisted himself up a fraction of an inch, just enough so his cock brushed my clit every second or third thrust. I thought that with my last orgasm I was done cuming for the night - I hadn't orgasmed this much in a 24 hour period in my life, ever - but I was wrong. The remnants of my last climax reignited, cutting the time needed to cum again to almost nothing. A raging fire burned inside me, cresting after another dozen rubs from the side of Jay's cock. "Yes," I screamed as I exploded again, the tone piercing my brain like a pickaxe. But what a pleasurable pain!

Jay's frantic movements above me broke into my orgasm bubble. I opened my eyes to see a wicked smile cross his lips. "I'm going to finally fill you up, Tiff." After a half dozen deep pumps, Jay collapsed on top of me. I wrapped my arms around his back, holding him tight to me. I peeled my feet off the dash and wrapped my legs around Jay's waist, drawing him even deeper into me.

We lay like that for many long minutes, both of us in no rush to separate. But eventually Jay softened and his cock slid out of me. I felt his juices slither out, running down my butt to pool on the seat underneath me. Jay pushed himself off me and, after a long, lingering kiss with lots of tongue, moved to the next seat. "Tiff, you exceeded my wildest fantasies of this moment." After a deep breath, he continued, "And I had some wild fantasies, let me tell you."

I laughed and reached over to squeeze his naked thigh. "That was pretty spectacular," I said. "You sure know how to use what you were given." That was an understatement.

"We should probably head back inside," Jay said, a touch of resignation in his voice.

"If we have to." I was reluctant to return to reality although I knew it was inevitable.

We both got redressed and adjusted our clothes. When Jay saw that I was ready, he said, "Wait there." He climbed out of the Festiva and came around to my side. He opened my door and I stepped out, my stiff legs enjoying the stretch.

Jay cupped my face and kissed me again. When he pulled away, he said, "I miss you already." He rested his forehead against mine as he seemed to summon his strength. "Once we get back inside, don't forget that we just met tonight."

"Got it. I'll lose the familiarity."

"Unfortunately, yes."

Jay and I hugged a tight embrace that had every inch of our bodies touching. Jay pulled back first, his reluctance to do so obvious. I let go of him even though every inch of me was screaming not to.

Jay took my hand and we walked back to the entrance to the club, neither of us going faster than a stroll. Having our time together come to an end was bittersweet.

Once inside, I spotted Liam and Sherry sitting on the bench where I'd first spotted Jay. As we headed their direction, I looked around the club. Hundreds of people were mingling and from outward appearances, they were all having a great time. I wondered about their stories and what had brought them here. If only the walls of The Swinger's Club could talk…

##########

The Swinger's Club: Chad and Lexi

I couldn't believe the words that came out of my mouth as I looked at my wife, Lexi: "I want to take a break from The Swinger's Club for awhile."

She looked at me like I'd sprouted a second nose and my skin had turned bright orange. "What?" she asked, no doubt thinking she didn't hear me right.

How could I make it clear to my wife that having sex with nameless strangers had lost its appeal? It sounded crazy to my own ears; I couldn't imagine how it sounded to her. I repeated myself, "Let's take a break from The Swinger's Club for a bit."

She looked like I'd stabbed her in a vital organ so I continued, "I don't mean we stop going forever. Just for a year or two." When a look of horror crossed her face, I said, "Okay, a few months." I reached for Lexi, wrapping my arm around her waist and pulling her against me. I buried my face in her neck. "You are all I need, babe."

I would've thought that would make her happy but I was wrong. She pushed away from me and stormed out of the kitchen. As I watched her back disappear around a corner, a flash of anger hit me. Unable to contain it, I picked up a coffee cup and dropped it into the sink, watching as the handle snapped off in one solid chunk. I picked up the pieces and tossed them into the trashcan as I contemplated the situation.

Over a year ago, bored with our sex life, I'd convinced Lexi to give The Swinger's Club a try. Our first time there, I'd spent two memorable and satisfying hours with a blonde with the tightest snatch I'd ever had. Lexi had clearly had fun, too, as her first question when I saw her after finishing with the blonde was, "When can we come back?"

We'd returned to The Swinger's Club the following Friday. And the Friday after that. And the Friday after that. And while I always had fun and got my rocks off, the novelty had long ago worn thin. It was the same every time. Lexi and I would prowl the club until we found another couple we wanted to spend time with. Lexi and the guy would go off to one room. The woman and I would go to another. A nameless woman and I would make out for a while and then we'd get down to fucking. There wasn't as much variety between the sex sessions as you'd think. I was ready for a break. Maybe in time I would want to return but for now, Lexi was all I needed.

Needing to work out my frustration over Lexi's reaction to my request for a Swinger's Club break, I changed into my running gear and hit the streets. I pounded out ten miles before I headed home; I was in no rush to return to the silent treatment. But that wasn't what was waiting for me when I slipped in the front door.

Lexi stood with her hip leaning against the kitchen island, my favorite after-workout smoothie in one hand. A grin that let me know she was up to something covered her face. I resisted the urge to ask, "What's up?" Instead, I took the smoothie from her outstretched hand and said, "Thanks."

As I guzzled the drink, Lexi said, "So, Chad, I've been thinking about what you said and I have a proposition for you."

The tiny hairs on the back of my neck stood up. Here it comes. I raised my eyebrows as if to say *Go Ahead*.

"The Swinger's Club has an entire private section designated for people like you."

I interrupted her before she could go on, "Like me?"

Lexi sighed before continuing, "People that are bored with the regular hook-ups."

"Go on."

"We can go to the back area that we've never been to before and delve into some harder stuff. Or you can just watch if you don't want to join in. I mean we can just watch."

I had no idea what she was talking about. Lexi continued, "So, here is my proposition. We go one more time to The Swinger's Club. We'll skip the usual crowd and go to the back area. If you still want a break after that, we will take a break. I'll agree to a break. For a couple of months at least. After that, we can renegotiate."

Now Lexi had me curious about the back area. And it probably wasn't fair of me to expect her to stop cold turkey just because I wanted to. "Okay," I agreed.

"Okay?" she asked, disbelief etched on her face.

"Yes, Lexi. I'm good with your proposition."

She threw her arms around my stinky, sweaty body and hugged me tight. When Lexi finally let go, she said, "I'll call and arrange it. I'm pretty sure you have to book a slot. This Friday work for you?"

"That'll work."

Lexi hugged me again. Just as my hands were about to wander down her back to cup her ass cheeks and grind her against my semi-hard-on, she pulled away. "I'm going to go call the club right now," she said.

She flew out of the kitchen before I had a chance to say another word. I finished my smoothie and aimed for our bedroom; I was in desperate need of a shower.

I was rinsing the underside of my balls when Lexi walked into the room looking like she'd won the lottery. "All good?" I asked as I brushed water off the glass shower door so I could see her clearly.

"All is more than good. We're booked in for Friday. They just need you to call them for some information."

Before I could overanalyze how Lexi would react, I swung open the glass door, grabbed her wrist, and yanked her into the shower with me. She squealed in delight.

My dick reacted instantly, hardening between our bodies as I pulled Lexi tight against me. I slid her robe off her shoulders. It puddled on the shower floor as my mouth attacked her neck and my hands groped every part of her that they could reach.

Feeling hornier than I have been in a while, I used my body to push Lexi back and pin her against the shower wall. I squeezed her ass hard before I grabbed her thigh and pulled her leg up so it circled my waist. Slipping a hand between our bodies, I angled my dick down so it was no longer pinned between us. The length of my dick rubbed against her pussy lips. Even with the shower water raining down on us, I could tell that Lexi's crotch was slick with pussy juice.

I bent my knees a few inches to line my dick up so I could stab into her. God, I was so close I could already feel Lexi's pussy wrapped around my shaft.

"Stop," Lexi screamed, the volume of the shriek startling me in the small space. What the fuck!

I pulled back so I could look at her face. She must've noticed how eager I was - why did she stop me? I should already be buried in her, my dick in pussy heaven. "What?" I asked, trying not to sound impatient; I didn't want her to cut me off altogether and have to jerk myself off.

"Bear with me, Chad. I need ten seconds."

As she slipped out of my grip and stepped out of the shower, my poor dick left hanging without so much as a pump, I clued in. Lexi had turned into a runner in recent months. She liked me to chase after her and catch her before I could screw her. Lucky for Lexi, that was a game I liked to play. Even better, her favorite place for me to 'catch' her was against the washing machine in the basement. Lexi didn't know this yet but I'd secured the washing machine to a base I'd built into the floor. Now it would be a hell of a lot sturdier when I was fucking her against it.

I gave my dick a few sympathy strokes to hold him over until I reached Lexi. I turned off the shower and dried myself before wrapping a towel around my waist. While I wanted to run to the basement, I strolled through the house and stopped at the door to the basement. "Oh, Lexi, where are you? I can't find you." I could almost hear her panting from up here.

I took each step into the basement as slow as I could go without moving backwards. "Where, oh where, could you be?" I reached the bottom step and took a left, heading for the laundry area.

As I rounded the last corner, I gasped at the spectacular sight in front of me. Lexi was sprawled on top of the washing machine, her backside to me. Her hands gripped the control panel at the back of the machine, holding herself steady even though she wasn't moving yet. Her legs were spread wide, giving me a glimpse of her perfect pink center. My dick was flexing wildly in her direction. This was going to be phenomenal!

"You found me!" Lexi shrieked as if she'd just spotted Ryan Reynolds, her hall pass.

"I sure did." I moved so I was directly behind her. Despite my impatience, I took a pause to admire the view. All Lexi's Pilates and Zumba paid off; she had a very impressive rear end. I slapped her ass hard and she almost came. This was going to be as easy as giving candy to a child. It wasn't going to take either of us long to orgasm.

I bent my knees, grabbed her hips, and drove my dick into Lexi's deep wetness. Her pussy squeezed me tight, already trying to milk my jism out of me. As we hadn't had sex in a few days and I'd been too busy with work to jerk off, I could've cum right then. But I forced myself to hold off. It wasn't easy. I held still for a few moments, relishing how awesome Lexi felt even when I wasn't moving inside her.

Lexi's hand slamming against the washing machine lid startled me, the metallic clang like a hammer to the side of my head. "Fuck me," Lexi spat out. "Hard." Her hand moved back to the console, gripping it tight in anticipation of what I was about to do.

My dick was happy to oblige. Instead of answering her with words, I pulled almost out of her before plunging back into her hole. I did it again and again, harder and faster each time as I got into my groove.

"Oh yeah, Chad. That's it. Fuck me baby!"

I loved when she rambled as I fucked her. She really was every man's dream - a slut in the bedroom, a lady outside of it. She was all I needed, in bed and out. I wish she would see that was a compliment to her.

"Baby, harder. I want to cum," she groaned.

I indulged her, our bodies slapping roughly together with each thrust. Good thing the washing machine was bolted down or we'd be moving all over the basement.

Lexi screamed as she came, her shriek loud enough to wake the neighbors had we been upstairs. Her core clenched violently at me, threatening to make me shoot my load. It almost happened but I held off, knowing my orgasm when it came would be even more amazing with a wait.

I didn't slow down to give Lexi a breather. I kept plunging into her, intent on dragging the fuck out as long as possible.

When Lexi had some strength back, she sat up on her elbows and tried to look back at me. I grabbed her ponytail and wrapped it around my fist, yanking her head back so I could see more of her face. "Like that?" I asked.

"You know I do. I love when you fuck me. Keep going, baby. Harder!"

I yanked her hair, knowing she liked pain when she was turned on. Her eyes glazed over and her hands moved to her tits. She was tweaking her nipples, the buds getting even harder. They stuck out from her body like two stumpy horizontal flagpoles. She was so hot.

I could tell she was building to another orgasm but I couldn't wait a second longer. I let go of her hair and clenched her hips, holding her tight as I plunged into her. Hard. And deep. I filled her up, hot streams of cum shooting out of me and into her depths.

Lexi tried to mask it but her sigh of disappointment was clear. She usually came two or three times when we got it on so one orgasm only must have felt like a letdown. Lucky for her, I'd planned ahead as I figured this day would eventually come.

I wasn't ready to leave Lexi's pussy - I liked to hang out in there until my dick softened - but I wanted Lexi to not backpedal too far from the orgasm she'd had building. I leaned close to her ear and whispered, "Stay there. Don't move."

My dick popped out as I moved to a shelf under the window. I pulled down a toolbox and opened it, taking out the vibrator I'd stashed in there a few weeks ago.

I returned to my spot behind Lexi's spread legs. "Hold still," I said, which was lame as Lexi didn't want to be anywhere but here. It would've taken a crane to peel her off the washing machine.

I turned on the toy and drove it into Lexi. Her entire body clenched up but she relaxed a few seconds later, embracing how good it felt as I moved the toy in and out of her. "How is that?" I asked, although the expression on her face was answer enough.

"Yeah," she mumbled. "That's the ticket."

I fucked her hard with the vibrator, harder and faster than I could fuck her with my own dick as my arm could move faster than my hips.

I thought Lexi would cum before my arm got tired but I was wrong. When my pumping speed started to slow, I knew a different angle would give my arm a break. I pulled the dripping wet vibrator out of her. I dropped it on top of the dryer, grabbed her waist, and spun her around. I picked her up and dropped her ass on top of the washing machine. I grabbed the vibrator and shoved it back inside her, barely missing a thrust.

Lexi rested back on her elbows and her head fell back between her shoulder blades. "Yeah, that's it," Lexi uttered to no one in particular.

Her hard, massive nipples grabbed my attention. With my free hand, I reached up and squeezed one of her boobs. Then the other. Then both at once, taking both of them into one fist. Lexi had tits that were made for fondling. And for fucking. My mind flashed back to the last time we'd had sex. In the seconds before I came, I'd whacked her tits with my dick and rubbed my shaft between her boobs. When I shot my load, I'd covered her nipples and tits with my jism. Thinking of that now, I rubbed her nipples between my fingertips so hard that it must've hurt. But if it did, it didn't seem to register with her; her face showed no pain.

As much as I didn't want to stop playing with her tits, my arm was starting to tire again. I slid my hand off her chest, down her abs, and over her mound. I zeroed in on her clit and tweaked the little bud. It didn't stay little for long. As I increased my pressure, it grew as blood rushed to the nub.

"Don't stop, Chad! Don't stop!"

Did she really think I was going to leave her hanging and go watch the game or something? I kept fondling her clit and fucking her with the toy. I loved the sight of it disappearing into Lexi's body. Ten minutes ago, that had been me vanishing into her depths. That thought was like an electric cattle prod to my core. Even though I'd just cum, my soft dick twitched a fraction.

"Harder," Lexi screamed, spittle flying from her mouth. Which hand did she want me to move harder? Instead of asking her, both of my hands increased their intensity. If I weren't careful, I would rub her clit right off her body.

"Yeah, baby. That's how I like it. More, more!" She lifted her left leg from where it had hung limply down the front of the washer and wrapped it around my waist. That opened up her core even more, giving me extra space to move.

I was about to call for a time out when Lexi screamed my name, her toes curling as she pinched the skin on my back. She had a whopper of an orgasm, judging by her body's reactions. Damn, I loved seeing it play out on Lexi's face when she came. Her eyes glazed over before rolling back into her head. Her lips parted and her skin flushed the color of a stop sign.

I kept the vibrator slowly moving in Lexi as she came down the other side of her orgasm. When she eventually opened her eyes again, I pulled the toy from her core and stepped to the sink to rinse it off before putting it back in the toolbox. "Nice call on that one," Lexi said, her words heavy with satisfaction.

"That fun toy has been in there patiently waiting for a day like today."

"You are the smartest man I've ever met."

Lexi was now sitting up. I put a hand on each of her thighs, giving them a squeeze. I kissed her on the neck and said, "I thought it was a great idea."

Lexi leaned toward me and pressed her lips to mine. "You never fail to surprise me," she said when she pulled back.

It was on the tip of my tongue to say, "That's why a break from The Swinger's Club is needed." But I stopped myself at the last second; no need to push it with Lexi since we'd come to a tentative agreement. I kissed her again to ensure I wouldn't speak.

Before things got heated again - I was now in the mood to drop onto the couch, zone out, and finish the Yankees game - I pulled away from Lexi and helped her off the washing machine. As we were going up the stairs, Lexi said, "Don't forget - The Swinger's Club needs you to give them a call today or tomorrow about our Friday booking. I left the number on a sticky note by your phone."

"Why do they need me to call?"

"The lady who took our booking said she needed to pin down your preferences."

"Okay. I'll call them tomorrow." Baseball and nachos were the only thing I wanted to give my attention to for the rest of the day.

#####

At work the next day, I closed the door to my office and dialled the number for The Swinger's Club. The woman who answered sounded like she moonlighted as a phone sex operator. "How can I help you?" she asked, sounding like she wanted to lick my balls.

"My name is Chad Underwood. My wife, Lexi, booked us in for something on Friday. She told me I needed to call you guys for something."

"Chad Underwood, Chad Underwood," she mumbled to herself as I heard her rifling through papers on her end of the phone. "Ah, yes, Mr. Underwood. You are scheduled for our deluxe special. You are a lucky man."

I interrupted her, "What is the deluxe special?"

"It is whatever you want it to be. The only limitation is your imagination."

That sounded like it should be the club's motto. "Alrighty then," I said.

"To make sure you get an experience you won't forget, I have a couple of questions for you. If you answer the questions truthfully, you will not be disappointed on Friday."

"Okay."

"We've heard everything and accommodated every desire here at The Swinger's Club so don't be hesitant about sharing with me things you've never told anyone."

"Okay. Got it. Fire away," I said.

"What is your deepest, darkest fantasy, Mr. Underwood?"

"Please call me Chad."

"What is your deepest, darkest fantasy, Chad?"

I thought about it for so long that the lady on the phone asked, "Shall we come back to that question?"

"Sure."

"Speaking strictly sexually, what is your ideal woman?"

That was an easy one. "Natural blonde, big boobs, small waist. And enough of an ass that you can grab onto it."

"Excellent. How do you like vaginas?"

Another easy one. "Tight and wet."

"Sorry, I should have been clearer. How do you like your vaginas landscaped in terms of hair? Full bush, landing strip, no hair, trimmed short all over…"

Lexi always kept herself trim and tidy so I thought I'd go for something else. "How about either a landing strip or fully bare."

"Excellent. What's your favorite lingerie color?"

"Black."

"Do you prefer women, men, or a combination of both?" Before I could answer, the lady continued, "To be clear, your wife will not be privy to your answers. This is between us and you only."

"Women only. The more the merrier."

"That's good. Give me those details. How many women do you mean? Two, three, four, or five perhaps?"

I thought about that. While five women fawning over me would be heaven, the pressure to give all those women a fair amount of attention would be too much to handle. "Three," I replied. After rethinking that, I added, "On second thought, let's go with two."

"Excellent. What are your thoughts on bondage?"

"For me or my partner?"

"Both. Let's start with you."

"I like to touch. I'm fine with being tied up for a brief time but I wouldn't want to be tied up the entire time."

"Excellent. Your partner or partners?"

"I do like for them to be tied up so I can do what I want with them. But again, not the whole time."

"Excellent. What about watching? Or voyeurism?"

The woman was getting annoying with telling me every answer I had was excellent. "Can you be a little more specific?" I asked. Her idea of voyeurism may be different from mine.

"Do you like to sit back and watch others get it on?" she asked.

Did I? I liked watching porn but that was because I had no other choice when Lexi wasn't around or if she wasn't in the mood. "I'm not sure. If I did watch, I'd like to join in sooner rather than later."

"Would you like to see your wife with other women?"

Hell yeah! "I most definitely would."

"Would you like to see her with other men?"

"Not at all."

"Just for clarity, you would get pleasure out of seeing women touch Mrs. Underwood and her touching them?"

"I would enjoy that, yes."

"Excellent. Moving on, how about gadgets?"

"Such as?"

"Whips?"

"No thanks."

"Flogger?"

I wasn't sure what that was but it didn't sound like my thing. "No."

"Nipple clamps?"

"Not for me. Fine for the ladies."

"Butt plugs?"

"Same answer."

"Vibrator?"

"Not for me. Anyone else can have at it."

"Excellent. Blindfold?"

"Not for me." I liked to watch everything.

"Gag."

"Not on my top 10 list."

"Cuffs?"

"Like with bondage? Fine for a bit but not the whole time. Not for me anyway. Fine if others want it the entire time."

"Munkey Barz?"

"What's that?

"Basically a leather belt the woman wears around her waist. It has handles that stick out both sides that you can grab for more control than just holding onto her waist or hips when having intercourse."

She made 'intercourse' sound like a surgical procedure. "Sure, I'd give one of those a try."

"Any toys or things you like that I didn't mention?"

"Not that I can think of."

"How about water activities like sex in the shower or in a bathtub?"

"No. I'm not a fan of chafing so I'll pass on everything water."

"Excellent. How about oral sex?"

"On me, yes."

"Anal sex?"

"No thanks."

"Excellent. Back to the original question, what is your ultimate sexual fantasy, Chad?"

"It probably goes back to what we touched on earlier. Two or three hot girls tending to my every need."

"Nothing else? We can accommodate anything, as I mentioned."

"What are some things others have asked for?"

"To be urinated on. Having a woman who is lactating. Cross dressers. Men wearing a diaper during foreplay. Being spanked or beaten. Controlled choking during climax. Men wearing women's clothing or lingerie. Role-playing. Dominance. Fetishes like feet or baby talk. Schoolgirl or cheerleader fantasies. You name it, we've heard it all and accommodated it all."

Holy crap - some people liked some freaky shit. I was probably putting her to sleep with my preferences.

She continued, "Hearing that list, would you like to add anything onto your fantasies list?"

"I'm good but thanks."

"If anything else comes to mind before Friday, call us back. We will be happy to accommodate last minute additions."

Damn, she liked the word accommodate almost as much as the word excellent. "Okay. Thank you."

"It has been a pleasure talking to you, Chad. Have a good day."

"You too." I hung up the phone and fell into my chair, my brain running like a hamster on a wheel. While I thought about sex a lot - hell, what guy didn't? - I'd never had to break it down and analyze it quite so distinctly before. The call had been unsettling while it was also a major turn on. My semi was testament to that. I wish I could've locked my office door and spent a few minutes on my favorite porn website so I could rub one out. Unfortunately I was already late for a meeting.

#####

The rest of the week flew by. I didn't think of our Friday night booking at The Swinger's Club nearly as often as I thought I would. But when I got home after work on Friday, it was impossible to not know that something special was about to go down. The house had an aura of excitement about it, cultivated by Lexi. She was fluttering around the place as if the Queen of England (or Ryan Reynolds) was coming to dinner. Or Brad Pitt. She was dolled up. I think she'd spent all day at the salon. Her hair was so big it added four more inches to her height. Her nails looked like talons. And her make-up had been professionally done. Don't get me started on the slinky robe she was strutting around the house in. She looked good enough to eat. I was tempted to toss her onto the kitchen table and chow down. But she was dishing out two plates of pasta so I knew my timing was off. Lexi was particular about her cooking and whatever she made needed to be eaten as soon as it was ready.

I inhaled the linguini swimming in Lexi's special sauce as we talked about our respective days. Neither of us had anything spectacular happen but I knew that would change later.

I cleared our plates when we were done as Lexi filled two bowls with berries and added a dollop of whipped cream to each. "Ready for tonight?" she asked as she sucked a blackberry off her spoon.

"I am. You?"

"Very. I'm curious to see how it will all play out."

"Me too," I admitted.

"I never did ask how your call to the club went the other day."

I knew she meant it as a question, not a statement. "It was fine. The lady who answered just wanted to know about my sexual preferences."

"Oooh, such as?"

"What I liked and didn't like. What toys I liked to use. That kind of stuff."

"What did you tell her?"

I reached over and brushed my hand over her arm. "You know exactly what I like, Lexi. There would be no surprises for you in any of the answers I gave."

She looked like she wanted to say more but she focused instead on a strawberry that kept running off her spoon. She chased it with military determination while I watched in amusement. It was petty of me but I got a great deal of pleasure out of watching Lexi squirm when she wasn't in total control of a situation or conversation.

The strawberry finally conquered, I asked, "What time do we need to leave?"

"Half past nine should be good. Our booking is for ten."

I looked at my watch. It was only 7:30. Lots of time for a long shower including a jerk-off session. Getting off now would give me more stamina later and I'd be able to get off twice at The Swinger's Club if the ladies were good in the sack.

I finished the last of my berries, put the bowl in the sink, and thanked Lexi for dinner.

"You're welcome," she said. "Off to relax?"

"Yeah. I want to take a long shower and take my time shaving."

She threw me a strange look but I ignored it. When she was in a weird mood, it was better not to question her about anything or she ended up in a puddle on the floor, unable to explain her tears. Instead, I kissed her on the forehead so I wouldn't smudge her make-up and thanked her again for dinner. I hightailed it to our bedroom. I dropped my clothes in the hamper and started the steam feature in the shower in lieu of water. I lay on the bench seat and thought of the night ahead. I wondered how many of the things the woman on the phone asked about that I said I liked would be a part of tonight. Just pondering it was enough to give me a stiffy. I grabbed my dick and stroked him, my eyes closed as I pictured two blonde babes ravaging my body.

"Want help with that?" Lexi asked from the other side of the shower door, scaring the crap out of me as I hadn't heard her come into the bathroom. I jumped up and let go of my dick. "Give me a heart attack, why don't you!" I yelled.

Lexi ignored my whiney words and repeated her question, "Want some help with that?" She pointed to my hard dick.

"I would love some but I don't want to ruin your hair and make-up."

Lexi opened the shower door and yanked me out of the stall. "Come lay on the bed," she said.

Following behind her as I left a trail of water, I flopped on the bed. Lexi pushed my legs apart and I spread them as wide as I could, my droopy balls hanging down on the mattress. She climbed between my legs and her mouth dove onto my dick. She took him completely into her face in one swoop. Lexi knew how I liked my dick sucked!

She pumped me ferociously with her lips and I didn't try to hold off my orgasm. As I got closer, I dug my fingers into her shoulder since I couldn't bury them in her hair as I usually did.

Lexi grabbed my balls and juggled them around the palm of her hand with the perfect amount of pressure. Damn, my wife had blowjob skills that never failed to impress. I needed to see if I could convince her to suck my dick more often.

Her mouth suddenly slid off my dick but her hand immediately took its spot. She stroked me so hard and fast that I exploded seconds later, a stream of jism shooting straight up in the air. We both watched it as it arced a foot above me before gravity claimed it. It splattered on my stomach. Another stream followed that one although it was much less impressive.

Lexi continued stroking me slowly until I was empty. "Thanks, baby," I said as she slid off the bed.

"Always happy to help." She leered at me with a hungry look on her face. And not for food…

"I'm going to be taking you up on that," I replied.

I rolled off the bed and wrapped my arm around her waist. "Want me to return the favor?"

"I'm good. I just wanted to give you a hand. Literally."

"That you did. And very well, I might add."

I was going in for a kiss when Lexi slipped out of my grasp, slapping my ass as she stepped away from me. "Get back into the shower, big boy."

I watched her strut out of our bedroom before I headed back to the shower. I let the water do its magic and I didn't get out until I'd emptied the hot water tank.

I dried off and took extra time splashing on cologne and getting dressed. Lexi came in as I was picking a tie and touched up her hair and face. "I'll wait for you downstairs," I said as she stood on her side of the closet rifling through her dresses.

"I won't be long, Chad," she replied.

I was mindlessly flipping channels when Lexi came down the stairs in a slinky red number. "Damn, you look amazing, baby. That dress - wow!"

I went to where she stood soaking up the compliments and kissed her cheek. "Sure you want to go out? We can have a kickass party for two right here on the floor," I suggested.

She swatted my chest. "You can have me all to yourself tomorrow. And the next day. And the day after that. We're going to the club tonight, they're expecting us."

"Okay, okay," I grumbled but secretly I was stoked to be going to The Swinger's Club. I had a hunch the night ahead was going to be unforgettable.

#####

For the first time in months, I was hit with a wave of excitement as Lexi and I stepped into The Swinger's Club. The fact that I didn't feel like I was doing a chore was a 180-degree switch from the last half dozen times we'd been here.

"Over this way," Lexi said, grabbing my hand and pulling me to the left. As we meandered through the club, couples we knew tried to get our attention. Lexi ignored everyone, acting as if she didn't see them. Then again, she did have tunnel vision for wherever she was taking us. I mouthed, "I'm sorry," to everyone that tried to say hello, although sorry was the one thing I wasn't; most of those couples could put me to sleep faster than a Bridget Jones movie.

We eventually reached our destination, a black door tucked away in the back corner of the club. The door blended in so well to the rest of the wall that I'd never noticed it before. Lexi knocked on the door three times and it opened, a big burly guy on the other side. "Can I help you?" he growled like a bear. His arms were the size of both of my legs put together. And I worked out.

"Lexi and Chad Underwood," Lexi said, not phased by the hulking figure.

Hulk looked at something on an iPad before moving to the side. "Go ahead," he said.

"Thank you," Lexi and I said in unison as we passed him.

We'd only gone a few steps when a stunning redhead materialized in front of us. "Lexi, Chad, follow me please," she said.

Single file like soldiers, we followed Red down a narrow hallway, passing eight closed doors before we came to one that was open. Red ushered us into a room that appeared bland at first. Until you noticed the hooks hidden in the walls and the sex toys lined up on shelves like knick-knack collectibles. A king-sized bed sat in the middle of the room, taking center stage. The only other piece of furniture in the room was a chair. "Chad, have a seat. Lexi, follow me," Red said.

After throwing a quick smile my way, Lexi left the room with Red. I plopped down on the end of the bed and lay back, my head hitting the mattress. I already had a semi just thinking of the night ahead. It was such a refreshing change to be excited to be here.

"Well, hello there," a woman said as she came into the room. Holy fuck - if I could've ordered a fantasy woman from a catalogue, the goddess in front of me would be it. With her massive pile of blonde hair, a big rack, and a tiny waist, she was it. Even better, she wore a black nightie that left little to the imagination. Her nipples were almost as big as dinner plates – I could see them clearly through the material - and I had an overwhelming urge to gnaw on them.

As she walked toward me, her thumb caught the hem of her nightie, pulling it up for a second. I caught a glimpse of her bald pussy and a tsunami of blood raced to my dick. I wanted that pussy. "Nice," I said, hoping she'd give it to me sooner rather than later.

"You like that?" she asked, lifting her hem again and holding it up.

Her bald pussy was a work of art. "I don't like it. I love it." I wiped the back of my hand across my mouth in case I was drooling.

"Ever been with a woman with no hair down there?"

"No."

"It'll blow your mind. I'll blow your mind."

"Prove it."

She laughed as she threw her head back, her big tits thrusting forward. Damn, she was smokin' hot. If they gave me an hour alone with her, I'd leave a very happy man.

"Not so fast," she said. "You'll get that and more but first things first."

She came to where I lay and held out her hand. I took it and she pulled me to standing. She slid my suit jacket off my shoulders before taking a very long time working on my tie, her nipples grazing my chest. I watched her nipples grow even harder, loving the view as I looked down into her nightie.

She finally had my tie undone. She pulled it free of my neck. As she went to work on the shirt buttons, I reached up and brushed her nipples, one of my thumbs caressing each of her nubs. When she didn't tell me to stop, I cupped her tits through the satiny material. Her boobs were full and heavy and filled my hands. I squeezed them harder than I should have but the goddess didn't seem to mind.

As I tweaked her nipples, I asked, "What's your name?"

"You can call me Candy. You go by Chad? Or would you prefer Mr. Underwood?" Her hand slid down my body to very briefly cup my package as she muttered, "...wood."

Her fingers went back to work on my shirt buttons as I wondered if I'd just imagined what happened. No, the heat that lingered on my dick was proof she'd touched me. "To answer your question, Chad is good," I said.

She peeled my shirt off as she said, "Chad, am I moving too fast for you or shall I slow it up a bit?" She dropped my shirt to the floor.

My hard dick should've made it clear she wasn't going fast enough. "You're good," I said. "Although feel free to go a little faster. I'm more than good with that."

Her fingers were running over my stomach muscles. "So you are okay if I undo your pants?"

"I am more than okay with you undoing my pants." I probably sounded like a wise-ass but I didn't care.

Candy dropped her fingers to my belt as I continued playing with her boobs. "Has anyone ever told you that you have nice tits?" I asked.

Candy smiled in answer. She moved from my undone belt buckle to my button and zipper. She made quick work of those - thankfully! - as I debated dropping my mouth to suck at her tits. But the chance was gone when she bent down to work my shoes and pants off.

"Have a seat in the chair," Candy said as I stepped out of my pant legs.

I did as she asked, now naked except for my boxers and socks. I yanked my socks off real quick, making a three point shot as they landed on top of my pants.

Candy grabbed a rope that hung from the wall and took a hold of my elbow. She lifted my left arm onto the high arm of the chair. As swiftly as if she'd been a Boy Scout with a rope merit badge, she secured my arm to the chair in three moves. She was repeating the same move with my right arm when another hot blonde poked her head through the slightly open door and said, "Five minutes."

"We'll be ready," Candy said.

As the other woman disappeared, I asked, "Ready for what?"

Candy grinned an all-knowing smile and said, "You'll see soon enough." She patted my tied arms, stood, and started walking toward the door.

"You're going to leave me here tied up and all alone for five minutes?"

My question stopped her. She turned around and slowly started walking back toward me. "What do you suggest?" Candy asked.

"How about a quick suck on those gorgeous nipples of yours?"

She pondered my question for a moment. "Sure. Okay. We have to make it quick." Candy didn't know it but I was the king of quick when I needed to be.

I finally clued in as to why the arms on chair I sat in were so high. Facing me, Candy manoeuvred herself onto my lap. Her legs moved under the chair's arms, her thighs resting on top of mine. She put her arms on my shoulders as she stared at me for a few seconds. I was surprised that it wasn't awkward as she was a stranger to me.

Abruptly she stood, her tits now in my face. Candy turned from side to side, her boobs slapping the sides of my cheeks. Her nipples hardened with each slap, jabbing into my face. I was in titty heaven!

I turned my head slightly, trying to catch a nipple in my mouth, even through the material of her nightie. But Candy was moving too fast. "Slow down," I said, my words muffled in her chest.

Candy must've understood what I was trying to say as she stopped moving altogether. She grabbed her own tits, one beautiful boob cupped in each hand, and pointed them in my direction. Her nips were less than an inch from my mouth! I gobbled her nipples, one and then the other. The satin covering her boobs grew wet as my mouth groped at her. I tried to push the material down with my nose but I had no luck. "Show me your nipples," I begged.

Candy was either eager to please or disgusted by her soaked nightie as she let one of her tiny straps fall from her shoulder. The material on her left side fell down, fully exposing one lush boob. I attacked it with my lips, frustrated when I couldn't get enough into my mouth to satisfy me.

When the other strap slid down her arm and the nightie pooled around Candy's waist, I gorged on her other boob. Candy smiled down at me, settling closer into my torso so I had easier access to her chest.

Zing! When she'd sunk lower, I could feel her pussy heat around my dick; he desperately wanted in on the action. I didn't want to but I pulled my face out of Candy's chest so I could speak. "Can you pull me out of my shorts? Just for a minute."

Candy looked at the clock on the wall. "A minute is all we have."

"That's fine." It would be better than nothing.

She looked like she didn't know what to do. "Please," I prodded.

She reached between our bodies and slid her hand into my boxer shorts. She pulled my dick free and gave him a couple of strokes. "Yes," I moaned. That was what I wanted. Actually no. I wanted her hot, wet pussy but a few pumps with her hand was a good start.

"You like that?"

"I do." The seconds were loudly ticking away. I wanted to be inside her so bad that my dick ached. "Can you sit on me?" I asked, sure she would know I was talking about my dick since she was already sitting on my lap.

"I really shouldn't. That's for later."

"You really should."

Candy looked at the open but empty doorway before looking back at me. "Okay. Just for a second."

I nodded, my mouth having gone dry.

Candy held my dick straight up and lowered herself onto me. She went slow, taking me into her one inch at a time. She squeezed her pussy walls tight as she sheathed me. She will be a great pussy to fuck. I chomped down on a boob to stifle my groan.

Candy finally had all of me inside her. She sat motionless on my lap; the only part of her moving was her pussy walls as she hugged me tight, released me, and hugged me tight again. Holy shit! I love all pussies. Big ones, small ones, wet ones, even dry ones that needed a little spit. But my favorites were ones like this that felt like they were having a seizure.

I pushed Candy's nipple out of my mouth with my tongue. "Can you ride me? Just a bit."

She took my jaw in her hand, clenching it painfully tight. "You don't get it. This is supposed to be the warm-up round. You know - shake my tits at you a little. Rub my butt across your crotch. Give you some eye candy. It's bad enough that I sat on your cock. I'm not going to ride you so don't ask again."

"Isn't this night supposed to be about pleasuring me? Isn't it about doing what I want?" I didn't care that I sounded like a whiny kid.

"You're right, it is. But all in good time."

"Now is the time."

Candy burst out laughing, her boobs jiggling seductively. Damn, I loved a good rack. "You certainly are a persistent one, aren't you?" Candy asked. She stood abruptly, my dick not happy about no longer being sheathed inside Candy.

"No," I said too loudly. "Come back!"

Candy straightened her nightie as she looked at me, a strange expression of genuine pity on her face. After a quick look at the doorway, she came back to me and dropped down to her knees. She took my dick into her mouth in one swoop. "Yeah, that's what I'm talking about," I mumbled to no one in particular.

Candy barely had time to fuck me with her mouth for a few seconds when we heard voices in the hall; people were getting closer fast. She stood, yanked my boxers over my dick, and bent over, her mouth inches from my ear. She licked her lips and whispered, "I wanted to taste my pussy juice on your cock. Nice…"

Damn, she had a potty mouth that I loved. I wanted to fuck her face so hard she wouldn't be able to say another dirty word for a week.

Candy stood and I saw Lexi and another blonde enter the room. The blonde was holding onto a rope. The other end of the rope was wrapped around Lexi's bound wrists; her hands were tied together in front of her. My attention was ripped away from my wife's hands to what she was wearing. Lexi had on a sexy black bra and a matching thong. She looked like a sexual vixen begging to be set free.

Candy interrupted my eye feast. "Chad, let me introduce Tawny to you. She's the one leading your wife."

"Hello," I said automatically as my gaze moved to Tawny. She could be Jennifer Lopez's albino twin sister with her big, blonde hair, pale yet perfect skin, and an ass that any living man would give his left nut to have the chance to slam into.

Candy went to Tawny and ran a hand up her arm before the two shared a hot, long kiss than left my dick aching even more. I glanced over at Lexi. She was watching the ladies with a look of lust on her face that I hadn't seen in awhile. I'd better up my game in the bedroom when it's just the two of us so I can see more of that expression.

The two women broke apart and Tawny came over to me. "It's nice to meet you, Chad. Are you ready for some fun?"

"I've been ready for what feels like hours."

"That's the spirit!" She looked down at my crotch, my dick sticking out of the top of my boxers. "That looks uncomfortable. Want me to free him?" she asked, nodding at my dick.

"Please."

As Tawny pulled my boxers down my hips, I lifted my butt up a couple of inches so she could slide them all the way off. My dick was relieved to be free although he was not happy that he wasn't getting any attention. "Say hi to him," I said to Tawny.

She knew I meant my dick. I didn't think she'd do anything more than glance his way but I was thankfully wrong. She bent over and gave him a quick suck, her lips squeezing me tight for a second. I barely had a chance to enjoy it before she stood and headed back toward Lexi and Candy. But she stopped halfway across the room and came back to me. She whispered just loud enough for me to hear, "Candy tastes good on your cock."

"Why don't you get the rest off?" I suggested. I was desperate for more action!

Tawny laughed, ignored my suggestion, and went back to Candy. The two exchanged words and led Lexi over to the bed. I thought they would lay her down on it but I was wrong. Tawny took Lexi's elbow and helped my wife stand on the bed. Then Tawny joined Lexi on the bed, pulling her to where the pillows sat against the headboard like ducks in a row. Tawny spun Lexi around so she had her back to the wall. Candy moved to a switch by the door and flicked it. A hook lowered from the ceiling above Lexi's head. When it was close enough for Tawny to reach, Candy stopped it. Tawny passed the rope through the hook and knotted it. Candy hit the switch again and the hook headed back toward the ceiling. Candy stopped it once Lexi's arms were fully extended above her head, the rope taut. Lexi now stood on the pillows, facing straight toward me. I loved how she looked, powerless to move and perfectly displayed for whatever Candy and Tawny want to do to her.

Speaking of the dynamic duo, they were chatting quietly in the far corner of the room. "Hey, Chad," Tawny called out. "Settle an argument for us. Should I eat Lexi out or should Candy?"

"Why don't you both come blow me and I'll see who has the better oral skills?"

Candy and Tawny looked at each other and Candy shrugged. Tawny made the decision for two of them. "Count me down from ten," Tawny said to Candy as she came to where I sat, bent over, and took my dick in her mouth. Her lips stroked me fast and tight and the ten seconds felt like two; it was over almost before it started. When the countdown reached zero, Candy's mouth replaced Tawny's. Her turn also felt like it lasted two seconds. Damn, I didn't even have a chance to enjoy either of them. "Well...?" Tawny asked as both ladies stood in front of me awaiting my answer, the ultimate feast for a horny man's eyes.

"Well, that really wasn't enough time for me to be able to make an informed decision. You both have skills. Lexi would be lucky to have either of you eat her out."

"He got us," Tawny said to Candy.

I wouldn't admit it to them but Tawny was right - I'd just wanted some dick action. Although the pathetically small amount they'd given me felt like a scrap thrown to a dog.

Candy and Tawny both climbed onto the bed. Tawny lay down on the end, stretching out like a cat, her boobs threatening to pop out of her nightie when she raised her arms above her head. Candy was crawling on all fours up the bed toward Lexi. I had a clear view of her ass and her muff from behind. My dick was aching - he wanted to spank that tight ass until it left a bruise.

Candy stopped at Lexi's feet. Her hands slowly crept up Lexi's body, goose bumps popping up on Lexi's skin where Candy touched. When Candy reached Lexi's panty-covered core, she skipped around that area and went right for Lexi's tits. After cupping her boobs for a few grabs, she tugged on two tiny tabs on the bra straps that I hadn't noticed. The centers of the bra cups peeled away, exposing Lexi's nipples. Her nips were already hard and sticking out from her body. I loved that Lexi was as turned on by all this as I was.

Candy devoured Lexi's tits as Tawny rolled off the bed and headed my way, crawling on her hands and knees. Her nightie hung down in the front, giving me a view of two spectacular tits. Was it a prerequisite for working here that you had to have boobs that most people only ever saw in a magazine? No matter how you looked at it, tonight was my lucky night!

Tawny stopped just in front of me, her chin resting on my knee as she looked up at my face. I flexed my dick, hoping she'd take the hint and give him some attention. She ran her hands up my legs, moving to the outsides of my thighs and clenching my hips. Holding them tight, she hoisted herself up to half standing. Her boobs hung in my face, just out of my mouth's reach. Being tied up and not able to touch was starting to get old. "Can you untie me, Tawny?" I asked.

Tawny flicked one of my nipples with her tongue. "In a bit," she replied. "Candy and I want to finish a few things first."

Her words thrilled and terrified me at the same time. "You can finish me off," I said only half in jest; my dick was in serious need of relief.

Tawny must have heard and agreed with me as she went into hyper drive speed. Moving up my body, she began gyrating as if she were a human worm. Her torso moved close to me and then further away and back again, her boobs in my face each time she got close. Damn, the woman had some serious moves. At one point, she grabbed the back of my head and pulled my face between her tits. I suffocated for a split second, her enormous tits engulfing my face. I loved it!

Just as abruptly as she'd grabbed me, Tawny let go of my head and spun around. She shook her firm, full ass into my lap. Her nightie rode up, giving me a view of her sexy rear end. My dick was clamoring to spank that ass. I tried shuffling closer to her as she was mere inches from my shaft but I had no luck.

Lexi's moans claimed my attention and I looked over Tawny's shoulder to see Candy chowing down on Lexi's pussy. Lexi's eyes were closed and her lips were slightly parted. A smile threatened to crack her face, Lexi's typical expression when she was in the throes of sexual bliss. I watched the back of Candy's head as she bobbed around in Lexi's core.

Lexi's moans grew louder and I could tell she was building up to an orgasm. I wanted to keep watching the Candy and Lexi show but Tawny grabbed my face, pulling it toward her. She was now facing me, her butt no longer twerking in my lap. "Ready to have your cock sucked?" she asked.

Finally! I looked at her lush, full lips and hoped she had great blowjob skills. "Yes," I answered, as if she needed to ask.

"Want it hard and fast or slow and gentle?"

I gulped. My mind was swirling with excitement. It was overloaded with all the action going on and I struggled to make my vocal cords work. "Hard and fast."

Tawny bent between my parted legs, her boobs resting against my thighs as she settled herself in for the job at hand. Speaking of hands, one of hers cupped my balls, gently tugging them away from my body as her other one went to the base of my shaft, pulling my dick toward her face. Without hesitation, Tawny swallowed my length whole.

My entire body reacted instantly. A violent shiver raced through me as I let out an embarrassing squeal. Thankfully the sound was drowned out by Lexi's moans.

I ripped my eyes away from the sight of Tawny's head bobbing in my lap so I could see what was going on on the bed. Lexi still had her arms pointing to the ceiling. Her bra cups were still open, her nipples jutting out. I'd been sucking on those nips for years but they looked reborn with the sexy bra framing them. I needed to get Lexi a bra like that for her to wear around the house; I would get off on watching her do housework while she wore it.

Candy was gripping Lexi's hips tight, holding Lexi steady as she chowed down on her. Lexi came a minute later, her scream deafening all of us. It sounded better than any symphony I'd ever heard, not that I listened to much Bach.

Candy didn't pull her face from Lexi's pussy until Lexi was almost recovered. Candy fell onto her back, looking up at Lexi with a victorious smile on her face. Abruptly Candy whipped her head to the side and looked my way. Her face glistened with pussy juice.

My expression must've shown that I wanted to lick her face because Candy made her way over to me. She tapped on Tawny's shoulder. Tawny's mouth let go of my dick so she could look up at Candy. "Switch me spots for a sec," Candy said. Tawny obliged, moving to the bed.

Candy straddled my thighs as she moved close to me. When she started lowering herself onto my lap, I flexed my dick hard. Candy impaled herself on my dick as our lips met. I devoured her face with my mouth and tongue. I was deep in the throes of tasting Lexi on Candy when Candy started riding me. She went slowly at first and then began picking up her pace.

I was so turned on that I knew I wouldn't last much longer. I was too worked up from all the build-up and the hours of anticipation before we'd even arrived at The Swinger's Club. "Slow down," I said as I passed the point of no return.

I bit into Candy's shoulder as I burst, my jism exploding from my body. Stream after stream shot out of me, likely filling Candy's insides. She squeezed her pussy walls around me, drawing the last of my juices from my body.

My head collapsed onto Candy's shoulder. Every ounce of my energy was sapped. She wrapped her arms around my shoulders, holding her entire body still as I fought to catch my breath.

I have no idea how much time passed as we sat like a pair of statues - pussy heaven distorts all sense of the clock - but Candy eventually shifted to the side and moved off me. I lifted my head to watch her go, my now-limp dick pooling in our combined juices in the middle of my crotch. Candy gave me a lingering kiss on the cheek before she joined Tawny on the bed.

The two of them started kissing as they played with each other's tits. It was all probably for show but what a show! They deep-throated each other, played with one another's boobs, and sucked the other person's nipples.

Lexi and I made eye contact. We grinned at each other like geeky teenagers, both of us feeling like we'd won the sexual lottery.

When Tawny's hand disappeared between Candy's thighs, my dick twitched a little; I got off on watching two women together.

I thought Tawny was going to finger fuck Candy but I was wrong. Tawny rolled off Candy and off the bed and grabbed what I'd previously thought was a piece of art hanging on the wall. Tawny unfolded the 'art' and a strap-on dildo was inside. She wrapped the belt around herself, the dildo sticking out from her body. She went back to the bed and rolled Candy onto her stomach. Tawny pulled Candy's ass into the air and spanked her butt cheeks with the dildo. "Do you want it?" Tawny asked Candy.

"I do."

"Are you ready?"

"Very. Hit me with it."

Tawny drove into Candy and proceeded to pile drive her ruthlessly with the dildo for minutes on end. It was mesmerizing to watch, my dick already getting semi-hard despite cuming not long ago.

Candy mumbled something. Tawny pulled out of her, flopping onto her back with her head landing between Lexi's feet. Candy crawled on top of Tawny and sank down onto the dildo. She rode the fake cock with as much enthusiasm as she'd ridden me not long before. To help hold herself up, Candy grabbed Lexi's waist, using my wife to pull herself up before dropping back down onto the dildo.

My dick was fully hard again; that's what watching three beautiful women on a bed would do to a man. "Hey, why don't you come over here and ride me instead," I said to Candy.

She looked over her shoulder at me. I thought she was going to say something but instead her eyes rolled back as she orgasmed. She was a quiet climaxer but the look of bliss on her face made up for her lack of sound.

Still sitting on top of Tawny, Candy spent a few minutes with her face between Lexi's legs before she moved. She crawled off Tawny and both of them sat up, one on each side of Lexi. Tawny and Candy each took one of Lexi's tits in their hands and progressed to sucking on her boobs. Lexi's head fell backward as her moans increased. I thought she was going to cum again - who wouldn't with two babes working you over. They continued their boob sucking as Tawny slid a hand between Lexi's legs. A few of Tawny's fingers disappeared inside Lexi. Tawny finger fucked Lexi with force and Lexi clearly loved it. But Candy didn't climax before Tawny's hand stopped playing inside her. Candy let go of the nipple she was tweaking and undid the strap-on that was still around Tawny's hips. Holding the base of the dildo, she shoved it into Lexi. Lexi's moans multiplied in volume as Candy focused on fucking her with the toy as hard and as fast as she could. Tawny took over the titty action, squeezing Lexi's boobs together as she sucked on both of her nipples at once.

Lexi came with the power of a sledgehammer. It rammed into her whole body as Candy and Tawny kept ravaging her. I thought for a moment that she was going to pass out but she was able to regain her breath when Candy pulled the dildo out of her body and gave her pussy a break.

I didn't want to make it all about me but now that Lexi had gotten off again, I wanted more dick action. "Hello, I'm over here," I said.

All three ladies ignored me. "Hello," I repeated, my tone a little sharper.

"Hold on," Tawny said, barely looking at me as she helped Candy get to her feet on the bed. Tawny and Candy each took one of Lexi's arms and undid the straps around her wrists that had kept her secured to the ceiling. Lexi fell free, collapsing to the bed. A look of sexual satisfaction was plastered on her face.

Candy sat on the bed next to Lexi, gently brushing the hair off Lexi's face as she took deep breaths. Tawny finally turned to me. She ignored my hard dick as she went to work untying my arms. She seemed in no rush whereas I was desperate to be free; I was fed up with not being able to touch anyone. I wanted to be an active participant.

The second my restraints were undone, my hands slid into Tawny's nightie. I grabbed her boobs like they were flotation devices and I was a drowning man. "Hold on there, big boy," she said, gently taking a hold of my wrists and pulling my hands from her top.

"What?" I asked. "It's my turn to touch, no?"

"Almost. Let's get you cleaned up first."

She dropped one of my wrists but kept holding the other as she led me toward the door. I looked over my shoulder at Lexi as we passed the bed. She threw me a lazy smile and a thumbs up sign. I smiled back at her, relieved she was cool with all of this. "Have fun, babe," I said to her and she gave me another thumbs up sign.

Tawny opened the door. A lady stood on the other side, a robe in her hands. She held it open and nodded her head at me. I took the hint and slipped my arms into the sleeves. "Maggie will take care of you," Tawny said. "I'll see you in a bit."

My dick deflated as I watched Tawny walk down the hallway away from me. Maggie was wearing what looked like a white doctor's coat and she inspired no sexual twinges at all. I followed her down a series of halls until she motioned me into an open door. The small room had a narrow bed in the middle of the space and nothing else. "Lay on your stomach, please," Maggie said.

I took off my robe and Maggie held out her hand for it, hanging it on a hook behind the door. As I approached the bed, I noticed a floor drain underneath it. What was up with that?

I found out the answer a minute later. I was lying on what felt like a massage table when water started dripping onto my body, hitting every bit of my skin from my scalp to my toes. When Tawny had said that I was going to get cleaned up, I didn't realize that she had meant it literally.

Maggie had a cloth of some type covering her hands. She proceeded to begin rubbing me down with it. As she was going to town on my left calf, I thought I heard the door open but I couldn't summon the strength to turn and look. Moments later, another cloth-covered pair of hands started on my right calf. I lost all sense of time as four hands slowly worked their way up my legs. I had a serious hard-on by the time they were working on my ass cheeks. To make it worse, my poor dick was pinned between the table and my body.

The four hands kept moving, giving me a full back massage before rubbing every inch of my arms. Having four hands on me was a turn-on unlike anything I'd ever experienced.

After my shoulders were rubbed down, one pair of hands set to work on my head. Damn - who would have thought that a scalp rub would feel so good?

Maggie spoke, startling me out of my zone. "Turn over, Chad."

I dug deep for enough energy to hoist myself up and flip over. The head rub didn't stop as I moved and it kept going after I was flat on my back. The water continued to slowly fall onto every part of my body from somewhere above me. The second pair of hands joined back in and my shoulders were tended to again. Then my arms and my chest. As the hands moved down my abs, I hoped they would finally give my dick a rub when they got a little further south. I flexed him a couple of times to get their attention although even if he hadn't moved, a stiffie would be hard to miss.

The ladies - I'd cracked my eyes when I flipped over to ensure they hadn't snuck a dude in here with Maggie and me - went to work on my hips. When they moved closer to my crotch, I figured my dick was finally going to get some action. Wrong! They continued down to my thighs despite my dick wagging at them.

I tried to focus on enjoying the leg message but it was hard when I was getting so frustrated. By the time they reached my ankles, I was debating giving myself a rub and tug.

When one hand touched each of my feet, I felt someone shuffle up to my head. A hand rested on my shoulder and Maggie spoke softly into my ear, "Would your cock like a massage, too?"

I nodded my head as I answered, "Yes. He would."

I heard more shuffling about and a pair of hands were placed on my stomach. The feeling of the touch had changed. She no longer had on cloth gloves; they now felt like a cross between gel and silk. My dick grew even harder as the hands moved in his direction.

The hands moved to my shaft and went to work. Hot damn, Maggie had serious handjob skills! It wasn't going to take long for me to blow my load again, especially as I wasn't going to try to hold off.

She stroked my dick and played with my balls as the other pair of hands continued to rub my legs and feet. I could get used to this treatment!

My orgasm continued to build as Maggie worked her magic. She sucked my dick as if her mouth was a Hoover vacuum and then stroked me with the perfect speed-to-squeeze ratio. She was a dick sucking and pumping master. When I was seconds from shooting my load, she must've known as she cut her stroking speed in half while still holding my shaft snug.

I burst, my cum oozing out before sliding down my length and into my crotch. The water continued to fall from the ceiling, washing away my jism as it seeped out of my dick.

The ladies kept going with their rubdowns, not stopping until my dick was limp and I was feeling refreshed.

The water shut off. I felt a blanket being settled over me, covering me from my neck all the way down to my feet. Maggie said, "Take your time getting up, Chad. We are in no rush. When you are ready, your robe is by the door and someone will be outside."

"Thanks," I managed to mumble.

I didn't move for many long minutes. I doubted I had been that relaxed in months. Not only was my dick satisfied, the rest of my body was, too. I couldn't feel an iota of tension anywhere.

I was almost comatose when I heard a soft knock on the door. A hand rested lightly on my shoulder. I cracked one of my eyes open and saw Candy smiling down at me. "Hey," she said.

"Hey," I returned.

"Tawny and I were wondering if you wanted to come and play with us."

My other eye popped open, too. Looking at her upside down, her rack looked even larger than it was. I could bury my face between those tits and stay there for hours.

I must've taken too long to answer for Candy's liking as she moved down my body, stopping when she reached my waist. She slid a hand under the blanket and reached around until she found my hand resting on my stomach. She pulled it free of the blanket and moved it to her crotch. She pressed my hand against her mound, my fingers sliding around the slip and slide that was her pussy. Oh, yeah, I definitely wanted a piece of that. My dick was in need of more recovery time but I had no doubt he'd step up by the time I needed him to. It had been awhile since I'd gotten my rocks off three times in one night - two was the norm during these nights at The Swinger's Club - but I was up for the challenge.

Candy moved away from me, my hand falling to my side. "Ready to join us?" she asked.

I sat up. "You know it."

Candy grabbed my robe off the hook and tossed it to me. I followed her out the door and down another maze of corridors to a sitting area. "It won't be long. We just need a few minutes. What can we get you to drink while we wait? You must be thirsty."

It hit me all at once that I was more than thirsty, I was dehydrated. "A big glass of water would be great, thanks."

"Anything to eat?"

I was hungry but I had no idea what I was in the mood for. "No, I'm good," I said.

Candy could see my indecision. "How about a small plate of nibbles?"

What the hell were nibbles? "Sure," I said, willing to give it a try.

"Okay. Someone will be right back. Tawny and I won't keep you waiting for long."

I watched her walk away, her sexy ass moving from side to side in a way guaranteed to make me lust for her. The fact that her nightie barely covered her tight ass added to the appeal.

No more than a minute passed before a sexy creature in a French maid's outfit brought me a large bottle of water and a cutting board that held crackers, cheese slices, grapes, and a pile of meats. "Hel-lo," I said, dragging the word out into two syllables. She was striking with her massive blue eyes, long blonde hair, cleavage that went almost to her neck, and a smokin' body that the outfit couldn't hide. I wanted to play with her!

"Anything else I can get you?" she asked.

"That is a very loaded question," I replied.

She smiled innocently at me, although I doubted there was an innocent bone in her body. She sashayed away, her hips swinging almost as much as Candy's had.

I ate every morsel on the board, washing it all down with the water. It all hit my system at the same time, a bolt of energy infusing me. That was exactly what I need to fuel up for whatever was in store ahead.

The lady in the maid outfit returned and said, "Follow me please."

As we wandered the hallways, I asked, "Are you joining Candy, Tawny, and I?"

"I'm sorry, sir. I only serve the drinks and food. I don't service the customers."

"That is a shame. I would have loved to take that outfit off of you and service you."

She blushed and I almost felt bad that I had made her uncomfortable. Then again, she's the one working at an establishment that promoted and encouraged sex....

"Here we are, sir." We stopped outside of a closed door. "Have a great time," she said.

I turned the knob and stepped into every man's fantasy.

The room in front of me was large. A massive bed took up one small corner. Racks covered an entire wall with every sex toy imaginable hanging from hooks. A tall, narrow cupboard held just one toy on top, the waist harness with handles that had been mentioned on the phone earlier in the week. Pommel horses in different heights stood throughout the room, I'm assuming to bend the women over when you wanted to fuck them from behind. I couldn't get over how many ropes, whips, chains, and devices were scattered all over the place.

I moved toward the focus point in the room. On one wall, Candy and Tawny were chained up, their hands above their heads, secured with chains that led to a hook in the ceiling. Each of the chains had a padlock on them.

"Well, hello, ladies," I said, my eyes feasting on the glorious sight set out in front of me. They both still wore their nighties and with their hands above their heads, the hems skimmed at their pussies. My gaze kept going from the fully shaved one to the one with the landing strip. I wanted to see more. Enough of the nighties!

I headed to the wall of toys, searching until I found a pair of scissors. Starting with Candy, I cut her nightie off. I started at the bottom, right at her pussy, moving the blades slowly up her body and through the valley between her tits. I was careful not to cut her skin. When I sliced through the lacy trim at the top of the nightie, the material fell open, exposing her perfect torso. Her boobs were spectacular and I took a minute to fondle them before moving on to Tawny's nightie. I cut hers in half, too, again starting at the bottom and working my way up. Her tits were even more amazing than Candy's and I lapped at them like a dog with a bone. I buried my face between them, pushing her fleshy tits into the sides of my face. I couldn't breathe but I didn't care. Now that I could touch the women, I was going to savor it.

I took the scissors and snipped the thin straps on the shoulders of both of the ladies. The shreds of their nighties fell to the floor, leaving them completely naked. As I stepped back to get a clear look at both of them, I knew I had really died and gone to fantasy heaven.

I moved to the bed and lay on my stomach, my chin resting on my crossed arms as I watched Candy and Tawny. What did I want to do with this opportunity? The women were completely at my disposal. Did I want to play with them for hours, fondling every inch of their bodies? Or did I just want to pound into them until my dick couldn't take it any longer? The ladies seemed in no rush for me to make a decision.

I ripped my eyes from the bald pussy that had claimed the majority of my attention and scanned the wall of treasures. A line-up of clamps of varying sizes looked interesting. I rolled off the bed and grabbed a pair of clamps off the wall. I walked to where Candy and Tawny stood, looking from one set of tits to the other. I'd never used nipple clamps before and I wasn't sure if they worked best on big nipples.

Tawny broke into my thoughts. "It helps to make the nipples hard first."

That I could do. Who would get them first? I opted for Tawny's pink, large nipples. I licked them both before pulling back and blowing on them, the cool air hitting her wet nipples and making the buds even harder. I took one of the clamps between my thumb and pointer finger and squeezed it open. I clamped it firmly onto Tawny's nipple and did the same with her other nipple. A thin chain hung between the two clamps, drooping down almost to her belly button.

I took a hold of the chain where it dipped the lowest and gave it a gentle tug. Tawny gasped, the sound half erotic, half painful. I did it again, watching the look of pleasure on Tawny's face as her nipples strained away from her body.

I let the chain fall and snagged another pair of clamps off the wall. I licked and blew on Candy's nipples and put clamps on her hard buds. Stepping back, I admired my handiwork. Damn, the women looked hot with their arms chained to the ceiling, their bodies bare, and hardware hanging off their tits.

I took Candy's chain in my left hand, Tawny's in my right. I tugged them both slowly but firmly. They reacted simultaneously, gasps escaping their lush lips. I got a serious woody watching their nipples threatening to pull away from their chests.

My hard dick was aching for attention. I left the clamps on the ladies as I pondered who I wanted to fuck first. I'd loved the feel of Candy's bald pussy when she'd ridden me so she would get first dibs. I moved in front of her so our noses were almost touching. I ran a hand down her body to cup her mound. She was already hot and I knew she would feel amazing. My dick was going crazy. "I want to fuck you so hard," I said to Candy. "Where's the key to the padlock?" I asked, nodding at the lock above her head.

"It's in Tawny's vagina."

Holy shit, that was hot! I smiled and said, "Great place for it."

I moved to where Tawny was chained up. I cupped and fondled her tits for a minute before one of my hands slid down her stomach and into her core. I circled her pussy lips with my fingers to lube them up and slid two fingers into Tawny's hole.

It didn't take me long to find the key. The tricky part was getting a firm grip on it so I could pull it out; Tawny was so wet and the key was slick with her juices. I managed to dig the key out on my third attempt.

Moving back to Candy, I said, "Open your mouth."

She did as I asked and I slid the key in her mouth. After she had enough time to get the juices off, I prodded at her lips with my fingers. She opened up and I took the key from between her teeth.

I undid the padlock and Candy breathed a sigh of relief as the blood rushed back into her arms. I didn't give her a chance to savor it. I took her hand and pulled her to where two pommel horses stood side by side; I had plans for the second one for later.

I bent Candy over the left one, her tits squishing against the leather-padded part as her perky, perfect ass faced me. Hell yeah, that was what I'd been waiting for! I rubbed my hands over her butt cheeks and gave them a few spanks. She squealed in excitement with each whack.

My patience snapped. I didn't want to wait any longer to shove my dick in her. I grabbed the waist belt off the stand and pulled Candy off the pommel horse just long enough to wrap it around her waist, securing it tightly. I kicked her legs further apart with my foot, grabbed one of the waist harness handles with my left hand, grabbed my dick with my right to line him up with Candy's pussy, and plowed into her.

She felt exactly how I knew she would - like I'd hit pussy nirvana. Between the pommel horse holding Candy firmly in place and the handles on the belt giving me extra control, I was able to drive into Candy with more force than I'd ever been able to do to anyone in the past. I was definitely getting a waist belt for Lexi and I to use.

I lost all concept of time as I kept fucking Candy. I would've been happy staying buried in her forever but I knew I would eventually cum again. Before that happened, I wanted a round or two with Tawny.

When I figured Candy was in need of a break, I let go of the handles and pulled my dick out of her. I gave my hands a shake, not realizing my hands were starting to cramp from holding the handles so tight for so long.

I picked the key up off the floor where I'd dropped it and undid Tawny's chains. As feeling flowed back into her arms, her moans were almost painful. Then again, I had kept her hanging up there for a long time.

I walked back to the side-by-side pommel horses and Tawny followed me. She went to bend over the horse beside Candy but I stopped her. I leaned back against it and pushed Tawny down to her knees. "Go slow," I said.

Tawny obliged, her blowjob skills any man's dream. She knew how to use her hot, wet mouth to keep me hard and engaged but not get me any closer to cuming; that would come soon enough, when I was fucking her.

When I'd had my fill of having my dick sucked, I bent down and pulled Tawny to standing, my dick popping out of her mouth with a smacking sound. I stepped clear of the pommel horse and pushed Tawny over it. Her ass was just as perfect as Candy's. I stepped back to admire the view of the two sexy asses waiting for me to spank and fuck.

I grabbed another waist belt with handles and slipped it around Tawny's waist. She resumed her position bent over the horse. Grabbing a hold of her handles, I drove into Tawny's pussy, my groans deafening all of us. That moment encompassed everything I loved most about pussies - they all felt a little different yet they were all glorious, a slice of sexual bliss.

"Oh, yeah, give it to me, Chad," Tawny screamed.

I fucked her hard, revelling in the feel of her tight, wet depths. I let go of one of the handles for a moment to reach over and give Candy's ass a slap. Her head popped up and she looked over her shoulder and back at me, a sexy smirk on her face.

I had an overwhelming urge to wipe that smirk off her lips. I pulled out of Tawny, took a step to the left, and plunged into Candy. I fucked that smirk off her face until she was gasping for breath. Then I switched pussies, fucking Tawny relentlessly again.

As much fun as I was having, I knew my dick was going to revolt soon; he wasn't used to quite this much action in one night. I no longer fought off the orgasm that wanted to come. I let it build as I continued to fuck Candy and Tawny. Playing musical chairs with pussies was a lot of fun.

When I knew I was about to blow, I pulled out of Tawny, aimed my dick straight in front of me, and shot my load all over Tawny and Candy's' asses. I watched, mesmerized as a gob of jism slid down Candy's ass crack, disappearing from view.

My legs threatened to buckle. I dug deep for the strength to make it to the bed. I collapsed on it, spread eagle. Exhaustion hit me like a semi barrelling down the highway at 100 mph. The past few hours had been phenomenal but also physically gruelling.

I heard the ladies moving around. I rolled onto my side and watched Candy and Tawny grab robes from a drawer in one of the cupboards. Candy was robed up first and came to where I lay. She kissed me on the cheek and said, "You were a lot of fun. I hope to see you again soon."

"You, too," I mumbled as she opened the door and left the room.

Tawny aimed for the door, blowing me a kiss as she went. "Bye, Chad."

"Bye, Tawny. Take it easy."

Alone in the room, I flopped onto my back. What a night! Lexi was right in planning this rendezvous to renew my lust for The Swinger's Club.

##########

The Swinger's Club: Amanda Worthington

I have a confession to make - I love cock. I love it so much that I've built my life and career around hard dicks.

Ten years ago, fresh out of a nasty divorce, I couldn't get enough sex. I would slip into bed with any guy that caught my attention. But more often than not, disappointment set in as I left their beds frustrated. Some men know how to work a woman's body like a concert pianist tickles the keys but for the majority of my past lovers, it's just wham, bam, that's it. No orgasm, no satisfaction for me. All the men thought they were stallions but they were more like mules.

I decided to look for a place to get guaranteed good sex. I did my research and discovered that there wasn't an established club for swingers within 200 miles. That was all the nudge I needed. I hadn't planned to own a sex club, only be a visitor, but that wasn't an option. I secured a loan, bought a cavernous building, and transformed it into a sexual haven. I opened the doors five months later and The Swinger's Club has been a moneymaker since day one.

While the financial freedom has been a blessing, the constant supply of hard cock and the never-ending sexual satisfaction is the greatest reward. It is a rare day that I leave for home and feel pent-up horniness - 99% of the time that is taken care of at the club.

From the outside, my life must seem mundane. I live alone. I don't even have a cat. I'm 35-years-old and happily single. I live on the top floor of a high-rise apartment. My doorman is probably the closest person to me outside of work. While most people would find that fact sad, I find it liberating. I work 12 hours a day, seven days a week. But as they say, if you love what you do, you'll never work a day in your life. That's me.

Take yesterday for example. I got to work ready to blow a gasket. I was so horny that leaves blowing in a stiff wind would've probably been enough to get me off. Instead, I remained calm on the outside. I changed into my favorite slutty outfit: a black push-up bra that made my smallish chest look voluminous, a thong that had the crotch conveniently missing, thigh-high stockings that stayed up on their own, and heels that made my long legs look like they would never end.

I had the interior of the club designed with my viewing pleasure in mind. There was a massive central area where couples mingled before going to private rooms in the upper level. The real money came from the private back area. It was a space that had to be booked and paid for in advance. It was a place where anyone could have any fantasy come true. It was also where I found my personal sexual gratification.

The maze of various sized rooms was where I always went when I needed release. Each room had a door with an inward looking peephole that was invisible unless you knew where to look for it. I stopped outside the rooms with closed doors (which meant that they were occupied) and peeked inside, making my way down the hallways until what was going on in a room appealed to me.

Yesterday it had been a room with Candy, one of the most popular girls who worked at my club. Candy had been busy servicing one of our regulars, Peter. Peter was a tall and lanky ginger, his limbs long and lean like mine. I knew from past experience that our bodies fit together as if we were two halves of one body. Even better, Peter had a cock that could fill any woman and he knew how to use it. Peter was a delicious man, inside and out.

I opened the door, startling Candy as she was in the middle of giving Peter a lap dance. "Hello," I said as I stepped into the room. "I hope I'm not interrupting."

Peter's eyes lit up as he hopped to his feet. "Not at all," he replied before Candy had a chance to say anything. "It's good to see you, Mandy." Clients were told that my name was Mandy, not Amanda, so customers wouldn't know I was the owner of the establishment.

"It's nice to see you, too, Peter. Candy, can I have a few minutes with Peter?"

She knew it was a given, not an actual question. Candy slid off Peter's lap and headed for the door. "You two have fun. I'll be in the red room when Peter is ready for me again," she said to me. Candy and I both knew she'd be kicking back in the staff room in her pyjamas and a pair of slippers but we always kept up the charade in front of clients.

Candy closed the door behind herself. I turned to Peter. Dang, he was a fine man. His muscles looked like they were barely contained by his skin. I walked over to where he stood and ran a hand up his arm, getting turned on by the feel of those taut muscles. When I reached his shoulder, Peter's hand jerked up and snatched my wrist. He pulled my hand toward his face and kissed the inside of my palm, his eyes closing as he did so. My free hand reached up to cup his jaw, his stubble poking at my fingers. A rush of gratitude raced through me that Peter was at my club at that moment; he was definitely ones of my faves.

"So, Peter, what brings you here today?" He knew that I was really asking what sexual fantasy he would like to have fulfilled.

Peter let go of my hand. "How about you just have your way with me, Mandy?"

"That's too easy. Aren't you in the mood for something specific?"

"Now I'm in the mood for your dirty mouth and your body riding me."

"That's it?"

"That's it. I'm easy to please."

I stepped closer to where he now sat back in a chair, closed the gap between us, and sat on his lap facing him. My thighs covered his. His hard cock was pressed against my core. I gasped, the sensation hitting me hard as the length of his shaft rubbed against my clit. I wrapped my arms around his shoulders and hugged him to me, his ironing board chest flattening my boobs between us. Peter wrapped his arms around my back before his hands fell down to my ass. He cupped my butt cheeks and squeezed them hard. I gasped again as his long fingers grazed my core as they dug into my flesh. "Hey," Peter said.

I pulled back and looked at him. "Yeah?"

"Why don't we take off my shorts?" Peter had on a pair of loose boxers, the only reason he hadn't slid into my depths when I sat on his lap.

I didn't want to leave my spot but I did want him inside me so I shifted backward and stepped off Peter. "Go ahead," I said after I'd given him enough space to take off his underwear.

"You take them off," he said.

I'd forgotten this side of Peter, the ornery, bossy guy that liked to give commands. Two could play that game. "No, you go ahead."

I would never let it show to Peter but his bossiness was a huge turn-on. I could feel my pussy flood with juice. But he had no idea, unless he could smell the tidal wave. I'd play hard to get as that usually pissed Peter off. When Peter was angry, it resulted in a harder fuck, the one thing I'd come into this room to get.

I turned my back - and my sexy ass in my crotchless panties, if I do say so myself - to Peter and went to a cupboard that was built into one corner of the room. I opened the third drawer from the top and pulled out a massive black dildo. I slammed the drawer shut harder than I meant to and headed to the bed as I ignored Peter. I sprawled out, spread my legs wide, and shoved the dildo inside my pussy.

I figured that would be all it took to smarten Peter up and I was right. He leapt off the chair, shrugged off his boxers, and jumped onto the bed. He ripped the dildo out of my hand and out of my pussy, moved between my thighs, and drove his cock into me. Holy fuck! That was what I'd needed since I woke up that morning. A pussy pounding could drive even the most tenacious tension from a woman's body. "Oh, yeah, Peter. That's it! Fuck me harder!"

Peter obliged, his body slamming into mine with the power of a life-sized drill. "Yeah," I rambled. "You know how I like it. You are so big!"

And he was. He filled every empty space inside me. With each of Peter's thrusts, I could feel my tension draining away. "Peter, that's the spot. I love when you fuck me hard."

Without warning, Peter pulled out, flipped me over, and rammed back into me from behind. "Oh yeah! You're the man, Peter! You are the best fuck I've ever had!" Okay, that was a slight exaggeration (although he was in my top ten) but saying dirty words spurred Peter on, giving me a more-fulfilling orgasm when my time came.

I slid one of my arms underneath me and reached back for my clit. I rubbed the tiny bud, my orgasm racing toward me even faster. It wouldn't take me long to climax in the mood I was in.

"Slap my ass," I ordered Peter. He obliged, his palm whacking my butt cheek, no doubt leaving a mark. "Again," I screamed, getting off on the burst of pain.

Peter slapped my ass again, even harder. He loved it, too. I could tell by the increased intensity of his thrusts.

"Fuck me harder, Peter," I begged. "I love your big cock driving into me."

My clit was swollen to twice its regular size. My body was silently screaming for release. I kept rubbing my clit as Peter fucked me ferociously.

My climax, as it always did, hit me with such power that it left me unable to breathe for a second. "Yes, Peter, yes!" I yelled as I peaked. As soon as I could breathe, I relaxed into the waves of release as they washed over my body. I was finally at peace. It didn't even matter that Peter was still plowing into me; I tuned that out.

I turned completely inward, relishing the release I'd been given. I loved having orgasms. I loved the feeling of peace and well-being that encompassed me afterward, sometimes for hours or, when especially appreciative, for days. I always languished in it for as long as possible. From a distance, I felt Peter climax but it had no effect on me.

As the last echoes of my orgasm left me, I let go of my inward pull and started tuning back into the world around me. I cracked an eye, looking up at the ceiling. Peter's weight was covering me like the world's heaviest blanket. While it was comforting, I didn't like to linger with clients once the deed was done.

I shifted to my side, rolling out from underneath Peter. "I'll get Candy to come back to you. Thanks for a fun time, Peter," I said as I cupped his face and kissed his cheek.

Peter mumbled something unintelligible but his satisfied smile said everything.

I left the room and headed for the staff area. Sure enough, Candy was there having a snack as she lounged in her robe watching *The Real Housewives* of some city. "Peter is ready for you to go back to him," I said.

Candy jumped to attention, quickly shedding her robe and slipping into a red teddy. "I'm on it. Thanks for the breather, Amanda."

"My pleasure." She and I both knew I meant it literally.

I went back to my office and closed and locked the door behind me. I stripped off my lingerie, dropping it into a basket near my desk. I opened a door that looked like it led to a closet but it was actually the entrance to my private bathroom. I'd spared no expense in the spacious room. The toilet and bidet were top of the line. The sink and marble counter had both been handpicked in Italy. The shower was my favorite thing, a glass-walled eight by eight foot square work of art. A built-in bench lined one wall and that was where I collapsed once the water was flowing. My bathroom was my haven, a place where I could be 100% alone with my thoughts.

After I'd cleaned up and redressed in a skirt and blouse, I planted my ass behind my desk and dug into my to-do list.

That had been yesterday. Today was a new day. I wasn't horny today but I was antsy. I hated being antsy, especially when I had no explanation for it. It was a frustrating feeling. Usually an orgasm or two was enough to banish it. In my current strange mood, I wasn't sure that I'd find anything that appealed to me but I figured I would give it a try.

Not feeling like full-on slut mode, I slipped into a white nightie, matching panties, and a silk robe that stopped halfway down my thigh. I went from closed door to closed door in the private back area, peeking in the peepholes in search of a situation that appealed to me. The first one I considered was a water room with a guy on a massage table. He was slick with water and his skin looked like melted chocolate. His dick was hard and huge and I knew that if I climbed on top of him, I'd be able to get off. But I doubted that would kick my antsiness. After debating the pros and cons of mounting the chocolate stallion, I kept going down the hallways.

I was about to give up and head back to my office when I peered into the only closed door I hadn't looked into. "No way," I whispered to myself. I pulled back from the peephole, blinked twice, and looked again to make sure my mind wasn't playing tricks on me. My naked ex-husband was in the room, his arms attached to chains on the wall. Two of my girls were whipping his chest and the front of his thighs with a flogger. Yup, that was definitely Harry. Oops, I meant Harold. He hated to be called Harry; he thought Harold was more sophisticated but I always thought of him as Harry. When I'd been married to him, he'd been a sexual dud. His idea of adventurous sex had been doing it on the couch instead of on our bed. I'd broached the idea of swinging with Harry once as I'd been desperate for action beyond Harry's boring five-minute routine. He'd shot me down cold. No way was someone else going to touch his woman, Harry had said. Little did my ex know how often and how thoroughly I was touched now. And by men a thousand times more skilled than he was. It's been years since I'd given Harry more than a passing thought. I'd been sure I was over him but as I watched him through the peephole, it hit me that I had lingering feelings of resentment tinged with anger. Even as I was disgusted by the thought of being near Harry, a tiny part of me craved a taste of payback. And I knew just how I was going to get it...

I knocked twice rapidly and then twice slowly on the door, my signal to the staff that I needed them. Cinnamon kept flogging Harry while Tawny came to the door. I motioned her into the hall with me, closing the door behind us. "What's his story?" I asked Tawny.

"Typical whip, dominate, and fuck until he gets off."

I laughed. "That sounds like most of our clientele."

"True that, Amanda. Do you need something?"

I pondered her question. Did I? Would Harry be the ideal outlet for my antsiness and newly-discovered resentment? While I'd been doubtful at first, it was probably the best antidote to my wonky feelings and mood.

"Do me a favor," I said. "Blindfold the client and I'll come in. You and Cinnamon can leave. Come back in 30 minutes."

"Will do, boss."

I watched through the peephole as Tawny took a sash from a drawer, approached Harry, exchanged a few words with him, and tied the blindfold tight. I quietly entered the room and walked to where Harry stood shackled to the wall. I signalled for Cinnamon and Tawny to leave and silently mouthed, "Thirty minutes." Tawny threw me a thumbs-up sign as the two ladies left the room.

I turned my attention back to Harry. It pained me to admit that he looked better now than he had when we were married. Where he'd been flabby and soft, he was now firm, even chiselled in parts. He'd aged well, his face almost unlined, his thick black hair untouched by grey. For some reason, that pissed me off even more. It would feel great taking my resentment out on him.

Harry spoke, startling me. His voice hadn't changed a bit. Too many memories, most of them painful, rushed back to me. "Anyone there?" he asked.

I had to be very careful to not speak one word as Harry would recognize my voice after the first syllable. In reply, I tweaked one of his nipples. Hard. His resulting roar held more pleasure than pain. I tweaked the other nipple even harder and Harry screamed with titillation. The man I'd been married to hadn't liked having his nipples touched. He sure hadn't liked having them twisted to the point of almost being ripped off.

To buy me some time to figure out what I wanted to do to Harry, I grabbed a whip and ran it over his body. I occasionally whacked him with it, which he clearly loved.

"Hey, rub my dick," Harry said, clueless that he was talking to his ex-wife.

I ran the whip over his hard-on. "Can you rub me with your hand or your mouth?" Harry asked. A few seconds later, he added, "Or your pussy…"

There was the crass guy I remembered so clearly. To his credit, he'd been patient long enough. If I were a guy, I would've wanted cock action long before now.

I grabbed a stool and placed it in front of Harry. I stepped onto it so I could reach the chains on his wrists. My tits were in Harry's face - I couldn't avoid it - and he tried catching a boob in his mouth. I worked as fast as I could, keeping the chains on Harry's wrists but freeing them from the hooks on the wall. He caught one of my nipples in his mouth and chomped on it. I had to bite my tongue to keep from yelling out. Instead, I circled his throat with one of my hands and slammed his head back against the wall. His skull made contact harder than I intended to. I would've felt bad had it not been for the lecherous and turned-on look that shrouded his face. Dang, he was more into pain than Tawny had hinted at.

Going with my instincts after years of dealing with masochists, once I had Harry's arms totally free of the wall but still shackled, I yanked his hands behind his back, holding both chains in one hand. My other hand took a hold of the fleshy part of his ear and used it to guide Harry to the bed. Once he was at the side of the mattress, I shoved him down on it. He did a face plant, hard. I could hear his moans even though his face was buried in the bedding.

I bent down and rolled him over, taking extra care to ensure his blindfold stayed in place. I raised his hands above his head and secured the chains on his wrists to the spindles in the headboard.

Standing on my knees, I straddled Harry's torso. I ran my fingers down his chest, feeling the thick muscles underneath his skin. Dang, he looked way too good now.

Harry thrust his hips suddenly, his hardness hitting my butt cheek. "C'mon," he said. "Fuck me."

The docile woman he'd been married to wanted vengeance. I pulled my arm back before sending it flying, slapping him hard across the face. He reacted by thrusting his hips upward again. "C'mon, do me." The slap had turned him on even more.

I stood on the bed and slid my panties off before returning to my knees and squatting over Harry's crotch. I slapped his other cheek at the exact moment that I sank onto his cock, my body startling me by remembering exactly how it felt to have Harry inside me. I skipped the warm up and rode Harry at top speed from the first second. The only challenge was keeping my mouth sealed shut as I was used to talking dirty, something almost all our male clientele enjoyed.

I was enveloped by a strange sensation of déjà vu. Memories of other times I'd ridden Harry came flooding back. That pissed me off for some reason. That made me want to punish him. I didn't like feeling anger as it spoiled my mood.

I slowed down my fucking speed as I reached up to undo one of Harry's arms; I figured I'd let him touch me. If I hated his hand on me, I'd tie him back up again. Extra tight. Circulation in one's arms was overrated anyway.

His hand free, I brought it to my boob. As he took over molding and playing with my tits, I let go of his hand. Dang, he still touched the same way - with too much pressure and no regard for the person attached to the tits. Another flash of anger hit me and I slapped his hand away. The whack spurred Harry on, his hand returning to my chest, fondling my tits even harder. I slapped his arm away, harder than I'd slapped his hand. That didn't deter him; his hand returned roughly to my chest.

What Harry said next turned my blood to ice and froze me: "You have tits just like my ex-wife. She was the queen of frigidness, a dud in the sack."

I dug deep inside and found my ability to move. I slapped his face with more force than I had before. He grabbed one of my boobs and yanked on it so hard that I almost blacked out from the pain. But my anger pulled me back. I grabbed his wrist and wrenched it above his head, reshackling his free arm to the headboard before he could stop me.

I leapt off the bed and took a ball gag from a drawer. I shoved it in Harry's mouth, securing it extra tight. I climbed back on top of Harry so I was straddling him. I dug my nails into the top of his chest. I dragged them all the way down his torso, leaving bloody spots as his skin collected under my fingernails. "Christ," Harry tried to moan; I could only make out the word as I knew his verbal nuances.

I slapped him across the face again, trying to stop his muffles. When that didn't work, I tuned his sounds out as I changed my focus 100% to myself.

Harry's cock was under me but instead of letting him back inside me - that was NEVER going to happen again in this lifetime - I lined the side of his cock up with my pussy area. I slid up and down the side of his cock, the length of his shaft rubbing my clit the entire time. I continued rubbing myself on him, ignoring Harry's groans as my orgasm built. I let it come full-speed ahead, my clit flourishing from so much attention.

I pursed my lips shut as my climax hit, surges of pleasure wracking me. It was a decent orgasm - not as good as most - but I still savored it, dragging it out as long as I could. But once I was over the initial phase of relief, a wave of revulsion hit me as I looked down at Harry. He was a horrible person, which is why I divorced him. I felt a sudden overwhelming urge to get as far away from him as fast as I could.

I climbed off the bed, leaving Harry shackled to the headboard. He was still blindfolded and gagged, his cock flailing about. I ran to the door. I must've been in the room with Harry for more than 30 minutes as Tawny and Cinnamon stood in the hall outside. I mumbled a thanks to them and ran back to my office, desperate to get every trace of Harry off me. I stood under the burning hot shower until I turned into a prune. Once dried off, I dressed in a skirt and blouse and buried myself in the towering stack of paperwork on my desk. I needed to exorcise Harry from my mind like I'd washed him from my body.

#####

It took almost a week to fully shed the negative emotions that Harry had brought to my world. Having amazing sex with a couple of my favorite regulars had helped, especially the romp in the room with mirrors for walls. Few things were better than hot sex to clear a person's mind.

One thing I loved most about my job was that it was never boring. Every day brought new surprises and challenges. That was a big part of why I loved what I did so much. I would shrivel up and die if I had to be a cubicle rat that did data entry for eight hours a day.

It was a chilly Tuesday morning when I received a call that really challenged me. "Amanda, it's Eric," said a familiar voice on the other end of the phone. Eric was one of my regulars. He was married to a gorgeous woman named Jennifer. Both were in their late 20s. Due to an illness and the medications Eric had to take for it, he was no longer able to maintain an erection. His doctors advised him against using Viagra and similar drugs as doing so in his condition could be fatal. Eric was a generous man who loved his wife. He didn't want her to suffer because he couldn't sexually satisfy her. Once every week or two, he would call me and arrange a situation for Jennifer that would pleasure her. Sometimes Eric joined in or he watched from the sidelines. Other times she came to the club solo.

"Eric, it's nice to hear your voice. How are you?"

"Great, thanks. You?"

"I'm good, too. How can I help you today?"

Eric hummed and hawed without saying much, which was unusual; I'd never seen a nervous side of him. "Take a deep breath," I suggested. I could hear him taking lengthy inhalations so I talked to give him time to calm down. "Eric, I promise you that there is no request that you can make that I haven't heard before. We've accommodated every sexual situation and every fetish that you can imagine."

I paused. When Eric didn't say anything, I continued, "I know you know this but everything here is held in the strictest confidence. This conversation, everything that happens in the club, any requests – every detail is confidential. You can ask me anything. I assure you there's nothing I can't handle."

I let that hang between us. When Eric finally spoke, he shocked the hell out of me. "I want someone to rape Jennifer."

To cover that his request had thrown me for the first time in a long time, I said, "Go on."

"Jen has always had a rape fantasy. I know it would turn her on big time if we could make it happen. So I was thinking your parking lot might work."

"In the parking lot?"

"She's always wanted it to happen outside for some reason. I figured the parking lot would be our best bet. What do you think?"

I thought about it for a few seconds. "Off the top of my head, the parking lot may pose a legal issue. But our options are limited if you want it done outside. I'm going to give our lawyer a quick call and I'll get back to you in about ten minutes."

"Okay. Thanks, Amanda."

"My pleasure. I'm always happy to accommodate your requests, Eric. I hope you know that."

I didn't need to call our lawyer. I just needed a minute to wrap my head around the ramifications of a pseudo-rape in the parking lot. By the time I called Eric back, I had a workable scenario in mind. "We have a private staff parking area on the opposite side of the building from where you usually park. It has a coded gate to get in. I will give you the code, you and Jennifer park in the back, and we'll take over from there. How does that sound?"

Eric let out a deep sigh of relief. "That sounds amazing. Thank you, Amanda."

"Don't thank me yet. I have one thing I need you to do before we go ahead with the plan."

"What's that?"

"I need to talk to Jennifer to hear for myself that she is good with this. When someone steps into the club, there is implied consent for whatever happens. Knowing Jennifer as I do, I have no doubt that she will enjoy the situation you have laid out for her. I just need to hear it from her." I would record the conversation to cover my ass.

"I'll get her to phone you as soon as she gets home from work."

"That would be great. I'll be expecting her call. When do you want to plan this scenario for?"

"Can we do Friday night? Around 11 p.m.?"

I flipped through our calendar of scheduled 'dates', making sure that Damian, the guy I had that would be perfect for this, was available. "That'll work. I have you penned in for eleven. Just make sure Jennifer calls me tonight."

"I will. And thank you so much, Amanda. I appreciate you always being so accommodating to the crazy requests Jennifer and I have."

"No need to thank me - you'll get my bill." We both laughed.

I continued, "But seriously, Eric, we are here to meet all your needs. I'm always happy to do what needs doing to ensure you and Jennifer have a satisfying experience."

"You're the best!"

"Talk soon."

Jennifer called that night. She sounded so excited about the rape scenario that I thought she was going to cum just talking about it on the phone. Clients such as Jennifer who were so easy to please were my favorite. Before we hung up, I made her choose a safe word - pineapple - although I doubted she would use it.

The next day, Damian and I had a strategy meeting and nailed down the details on how we'd pull off the pseudo-rape. By the time we finalized the plans, I was 100% confident that it would go off with no issues. "Thanks, Damian. If I haven't told you recently, I appreciate how much of a team player you are. I won't forget that during your yearly review next month. You can expect a substantial raise." Damian had worked for me since I opened the club and had quickly become one of my most dependable staff members. And he was very popular with the ladies.

"No problem, Amanda. I'm always happy to pitch in where needed, as you know." An odd note in his voice caused me to look up from the papers on my desk. Damian was too good looking. He should've been a statue on display at the Metropolitan Museum of Art. To say he'd hit the gene lottery was an understatement. That on top of how well he took care of his body left him almost hard to look at. Then again, anyone who could make Channing Tatum look like a five was impressive. But it wasn't just his appearance; he had charm and charisma that oozed from every pore.

"Is there something else?" I asked.

"May I speak frankly?" Damian asked.

I put down my pen and stepped to the side of the desk closest to him. I leaned against the edge of it, my hands resting on either side of my butt. "Damian, you have become an invaluable employee to me. I don't take that lightly. I hope you know that my door is always open for you about anything."

He bit his lip, clearly torn as to whether to speak his mind. "Spit it out," I said.

"Okay. Here goes. Will you go on a date with me?"

That was the last thing I'd expected to come out of his sexy mouth. Dang - that was one too many surprises in one week. At least it was a pleasant one. I would admit to myself but never to Damian that he'd been in more than one of my fantasies when I masturbated. It would be impossible not to think of him sexually when I needed inspiration. It was no surprise that he always received top ratings from our clients when they filled out comment cards.

"In another lifetime, I would love to go on a date with you," I replied. "But I have to say no for two reasons. One, I am almost old enough to be your mother."

Damian interrupted me. "No, that's not true. Maybe my big sister but not my mother." That was close enough. I was 35 and he would be 25 next month.

"Semantics," I said.

"Number two?" Damian asked.

"Two, I never date my staff. That's a rule I've never broken and I never plan to. It would end badly. It always does. I've seen it too many times. And I would hate to lose you when that happened."

Damian stood and came to where I rested against the desk. He cupped my jaw with his hands and I couldn't stop myself from pressing my cheek against his palm. His simple touch felt more intimate than most sex sessions I'd had lately. He spoke first, "Amanda, age is only a number so get that ridiculous excuse out of your mind. As for your second argument, it's just a date. One date. I'm not asking you to marry me. A date. You know, I pick you up, take you for dinner. We go bowling or to a movie. A date."

The intimacy of his touch and the words Damian said unnerved me. I couldn't seem to catch my breath. I playfully pushed him away to break his contact with me and walked around to the other side of the desk; I needed to put some distance between us so I could breathe again. "Let me think about it," I said, dismissing him.

"I'll stop by tomorrow and see what you decided."

"Okay," I agreed, suddenly desperate for him to leave.

Thankfully, he took the hint and headed for the door. But before he left, he smiled my way and blew me a kiss. I threw a pencil at him, barely missing his head before he shut the door.

Damian. Dang. What was I going to do with him? I never date my staff, that was true. But what I'd left unsaid was that I didn't date staff as no one had ever appealed to me before Damian. Wisdom told me to turn him down and make it clear that he was never to ask me out again. But there was a tiny part of me that was tempted to say yes. Damian put on a tough guy exterior but he was the kind of guy who would help an old lady cross the street, even if it took ten minutes to get from one side to the other. Then he would go home and ravage the lucky woman who was waiting for him. He would give her multiple orgasms before he addressed his own needs.

I shook my head, trying to brush away thoughts of Damian. Too bad it wasn't that easy. Instead I turned to the paperwork that I needed to complete for Jennifer's rape scenario. That was going down in two days.

#####

Usually a man being true to his word was a desirable trait but when Damian stopped at my office the following evening, I had to work to stifle my groan.

"Hey, Amanda. I said I'd check in with you tonight and see if you had a chance to decide on my date idea…"

I closed the lid on my laptop and walked to where Damian hovered a step inside my office door. "I'm going to be honest with you. As you know, I don't typically participate in the requests that our clients ask us to fill."

Damian interrupted, "I know that. But what does that have to do with me taking you to dinner and a movie?"

"If you remember our strategy meeting for Jennifer tomorrow night, you'll recall that I am going to do that with you."

"I remember that very well. I'm looking forward to it," Damian said.

I smiled at his cheekiness. "Well, good. I'm glad to hear that. Anyway, my mind is so filled with thoughts of tomorrow night that I haven't had a chance to think of anything else. I'm nervous about tomorrow actually. While we've done and seen almost everything here, tomorrow night will be a first. What I'm getting at is that I haven't had a chance to properly consider going on a date with you. So, in a roundabout way I'm asking if you'll give me until the weekend to give you an answer. I just want to get through tomorrow night."

Damian grinned at me, a look that was filled with something that I couldn't quite decipher. "Sure, I'll give you until the weekend. I want to be clear that I hope your answer will be yes."

"Noted. I'm giving your request the consideration it deserves so I appreciate you giving me the extra time," I said.

"No need to sound so formal."

I ignored his sarcasm. "Anyway, about tomorrow night, you all squared away? Do you want to go over any details?"

"Nope. I've already been to wardrobe and that's lined up. I'll meet you by the door to the staff parking lot at ten to eleven."

"I've made it clear to Eric that he can't be early, he needs to pull into the lot at eleven sharp. So 10:50 will work."

"Excellent. I'll see you then."

"Anything else you need to go over?" I asked. I knew he was booked with a full night of activities for the next five hours and only had a minute until he needed to get to work.

"I'm good." Damian left the room without mentioning our possible date again.

It was strange - the space felt oddly empty without him in it. Pushing the feeling aside, I fired my laptop up and turned my attention to the financial spreadsheet I'd been working on. But I was having serious trouble focusing. I finally gave up when I knew getting my financials up to date was futile.

I pulled up that night's schedule to see where Damian was. For the next 25 minutes, he was in room 3C. Without wasting time pondering what I was doing, I left my office.

When I reached the door to 3C, I hesitated before looking in the peephole. It was tough to admit to myself that I wasn't there solely to check up on a staff member. I wanted a glimpse of Damian when he wouldn't be watching me in return; I always felt like a bug under a microscope when he turned his sky blue eyes in my direction. "Stop, Amanda," I chastised myself. Before I could completely overanalyze what I was doing, I stood on my tiptoes and looked through the peephole.

Damian was on the bed with two women. He was giving both of them his full attention, having at least a hand - or his cock - on each of them at all times. That's what Damian excelled at: making whoever he was with feel like they were the only thing in the world that mattered.

Watching him work, I questioned whether I could date someone who had sex with people for a living. I knew that was hypocritical of me as I pretty much slept with whoever I wanted, whenever I wanted. That fact wasn't even touching on the other issue - our age differences. I wasn't sure I was okay with the ten-year age gap.

Damian suddenly turned and looked directly at me. I jumped back even though I knew it was impossible that he had seen me; the peepholes were designed to be one-way only. Damian wouldn't even have been able to see a shadow. Realizing I was being ridiculous, I put my eye back up to the door and looked into the room. Damian had resumed fucking one of the women. Watching him felt wrong. I made myself peel my eyes away from Damian's spectacular body and go follow up on actual staff issues.

#####

I couldn't have ordered better weather on Friday for Jennifer's pseudo-rape. The day was warm and clear and the temperatures wouldn't drop off much before eleven.

Half an hour before I was to meet Damian near the parking lot, I rifled through my wardrobe for my black jeggings. I slid them on before taking off my blouse and replacing it with a black turtleneck. I brushed my hair back and into a low ponytail, securing it extra tight with bobby pins around the hair tie. I debated adding a black pair of gloves but that seemed like overkill.

At ten to eleven, I was at the door to the parking lot. Damian showed up 30 seconds later, smiling crookedly at me as he drew closer. My heart skipped a beat. And then skipped another. I'd always been aware that Damian was off the hotness scale but for some reason, tonight he looked so attractive that I was intimidated. I blushed deeply, grateful that the hall lighting wouldn't give my redness away.

"Amanda," Damian said as he bent down to kiss my cheek.

"Damian," I replied, making the mistake of inhaling as he drew close to me. My nose registered a healthy dose of his aftershave. No man had ever smelled better and I'd smelled my share of men. "Nice aftershave," I said, unable to stop myself.

Damian surprised me by wrapping his arms around my back and dipping me so my head was almost touching the ground. He cupped the back of my head, pulling my face into the crook of his neck. "Take a good whiff," he said.

Dang, I could barely breathe. Being in Damian's orbit was overwhelming. To mask my discomfort, I swatted him away the best I could manage with my elbows pinned to my sides. "Let me go, you big goof," I ordered.

He brought me to my feet and let me go with a flourish. "Goof? Did you really just call me a goof? Who over the age of ten calls anyone a goof?"

I cut him off. Trying not to laugh, I said, "Let's get to work in case they get here soon."

Damian threw me a mock salute. "Yes, ma'am. At your service, ma'am..."

"God, you make me feel so old when you call me ma'am."

"Go on a date with me and I promise you'll feel young and frisky."

"Enough. Let's go," I said. I put on a cranky facade but inside I was thrilled with his banter. Damian brought out a fun side in me that I didn't have enough of in my life.

Damian opened the door to the parking lot and gestured for me to go ahead of him. I stepped outside. The moon was full and bright, providing more than enough light to see when combined with the motion-sensor lights I'd had installed. We were using Tawny's beat up Mazda 3 as the staging area. The car was full of hail dents and an assortment of dings from her numerous fender benders; Tawny claimed any additional dents wouldn't be noticed. The Mazda was in the second stall from the furthest back corner as we'd asked of her. Eric had been instructed to park in the last stall, next to the Mazda.

We ducked down behind the trunk of the car - Tawny had backed in - and glued our eyes to the gated entrance. "Ready for this?" Damian asked.

"I am. But I'll admit I'm a little nervous. We've never done anything outside of the club like this."

"Don't you worry; it'll go off without a hitch. Jennifer is quick to please so we probably won't be out here more than five minutes anyway."

I laughed. "Good point."

Looking down Damian's long, buff body, I said, "Wardrobe did a great job on your outfit."

He looked down at himself as if he'd forgotten what he was wearing. He had on a black t-shirt that he looked about to burst out of, a pair of black athletic pants, a black bandana around his neck, and a black baseball cap turned backwards but pulled down low on his forehead. "I'm not quite ready for a date at the opera with you but it'll do for now," he said.

Damian wasn't going to let it go. I swatted his arm to avoid having to say anything in response.

"Do you like the opera?" Damian asked.

"Really? You are asking me this now?"

"I'm just passing the time until Eric and Jennifer get here. I really don't know much about who you are as a person."

I grumbled something unintelligible in reply. I was antsy and wanted to crawl out of my own skin. I didn't want to talk about Madame Butterfly or La Boheme. If Eric and Jennifer would just arrive, Damian and I could get to work instead of sitting here doing nothing.

I stood and paced behind the car. Damian stood and grabbed a hold of my waist the next time I passed him. "I've got this, Amanda, if you want to go inside."

"I'm not leaving you out here alone," I said.

"I'll be fine. Besides, you aren't any help in your anxious condition."

I shook off his hand. "I'm not anxious. I'm fine," I huffed even though we both knew I wasn't.

Damian wrapped his arms around me and dipped me like he'd done by the door. "I really want to kiss you," he said. "May I?"

What the hell? He was probably trying to distract me from my mood but I wasn't feeling it. "I think I'm good," I said.

"Is that a yes or a no?"

"Damian, stop trying to piss me off!"

"That's not what I'm trying to do. All I want is to kiss you."

Dang, his eyes were like deep pools of ocean water. I couldn't pull my gaze away from them. And, for some reason, my vocal cords seemed to stop working when my eyes locked on his.

Damian filled the silence, "It'll be a light kiss. No pressure on you. No tongue unless you initiate it."

I was trying to say, "Okay," when we heard the gate start to swing open. Damian cupped my elbow, steadying me. We ducked down at the same time, just before Eric's headlights would have spotlighted us. "Shh," I said even though neither of us was making a sound other than me shushing us.

Damian squeezed my shoulder, some of his strength flowing into my body and calming me. "It's going to be okay," Damian mouthed silently.

I nodded at him with more confidence than I felt. What was wrong with me? I was usually a self-assured person. A handsome man and a new scenario typically made me thrive, it didn't throw me off my game. I needed to pull myself together. I probably just needed a thorough fucking.

Eric was the slowest driver in the history of man but he did eventually manage to get his car into the designated parking spot and turn off the engine. As we'd prearranged, Eric was to stay in his car until it was over and I knocked on his window. Jennifer would get out and walk toward the door.

Damian and I were hiding behind the Mazda so we were able to hear them but not see them. Jennifer had no clue where we were. Eric and Jennifer said good-bye as casually as if Eric was dropping her off to do errands. Jennifer slammed the passenger door shut and I peeked up to see her ambling away from Eric's car.

Damian looked over at me and I nodded. He took a second to lean back and give me a quick kiss that was over before I had a chance to react, throwing me off balance for a moment. By the time I'd recovered and tried to swat him, he was crossing the parking lot and rapidly approaching Jennifer from behind.

Damian snatched Jennifer off her feet. He wrapped one arm around her waist, the other around her shoulders so his hand could clamp down on her mouth. Jennifer's muffled screams jarred me into action. I raced to where they stood, picking up Jennifer's purse and tossing it onto the hood of Eric's car. By then Damian had pulled Jennifer to the back of the Mazda. He slammed her hard against the trunk, her stomach plastered against the metal. He pushed her arms against the car and I jumped in to do my part - holding her arms straight out on the trunk so Jennifer couldn't move her top half.

Jennifer was wearing a long-sleeved blouse and a knee length skirt. Damian flipped her skirt up so it lay on her back. From my spot on the opposite side of the car, I couldn't see if Jennifer was wearing anything under her skirt. Damian's eyes were going ballistic roaming over her ass. Jennifer probably had an impressive butt. Damian slapped her ass cheek hard and bent over so he was laying on top of her, his crotch pressing into her butt. He moved his mouth close to her ear. "Shut up," he whispered. "Shut your mouth." Her screams turned to moans, which were still deafening in the quiet night.

Damian stood and reached between Jennifer's legs. He yanked hard, ripping off a pair of hot pink panties. He bent over Jennifer again and shoved her underwear in her mouth, stifling her moans.

Damian reached into his pants and pulled out his hard cock. Holy crap - it was even bigger up close. He was huge and would fill even the biggest pussy. Using his knees, he kicked Jennifer's legs apart, spreading them even wider. He spit into his hand and rubbed his cock before ramming into Jennifer's body.

Jennifer bucked wildly, her head raring back as she was impaled. Our eyes connected briefly when her head came up. In that glance, all my doubts concerning this fake rape were washed away. Jennifer was loving every second of this. Damian probably didn't even need the saliva.

Jennifer's body shook the car as Damian pounded into her over and over again. I avoided looked at him, uncomfortable so close to him when he was fucking someone else.

I held tight to Jennifer's arms although she wasn't resisting. When she looked up at me a second time, I whispered, "Pineapple?" She shook her head violently.

Damian grabbed Jennifer's ponytail and yanked her head up. His teeth clenched, he said, "I said shut up, bitch. So shut the fuck up. Now." He shoved her head down so hard that her forehead connected with the metal, undoubtedly leaving a goose egg. A part of me wanted to tell Damian to be more careful but it was more than obvious that Jennifer didn't want a light touch.

Going off script, Damian pulled Jennifer so hard off the car that her arms slipped out of my grip. He looked at her and pointed at the treed area behind the parking lot. "Go. Run," he yelled.

Jennifer looked torn, unsure what to do. Damian pointed again. "You have five seconds. Run!" She took off like a spooked deer, quickly disappearing into the shrubbery.

I glanced over at Damian. "That's a great look for you," I said to him. With the bandana covering most of his face and his body fully covered except for his arms and his rock hard cock sticking out of his pants, he looked comical.

"You want a turn?" Damian asked, a tinge of crudeness in his voice.

"I'm good," I said, holding my hands up in surrender.

Damian took off after Jennifer and I followed, never more than two steps behind. She hadn't gotten as far as I thought she would. Damian tackled her, both of them landing in a pile of leaves that were on the cusp of rotting. Damian rolled Jennifer onto her back and moved so he was between her legs. Without a pause, he drove his cock into her.

I didn't know what to do now that I was not needed there. I felt like a perverted voyeur standing behind them. Jennifer wasn't fighting Damian off but I grabbed her arms anyway. I pulled them over her head and held them against the ground. She'd spit her panties out of her mouth sometime during her run so her screams of excitement hit my ears hard. I was debating taking off my own panties to shove in her mouth when Damian yanked off his bandana and tossed it at me. "Shut her up," he said to me. I let go of one of Jennifer's arms just long enough for me to gag her again.

Using one hand to hold Jennifer's hip steady, his other one moved to her chest. He grabbed her blouse in one fist and ripped the entire thing off. He yanked her bra off her body and tossed it into a bush. He clutched at her tits so hard that it had to have hurt but it just spurred Jennifer on. The woman was so horny and worked up that she was about to either cum or have a seizure.

Damian pinched Jennifer's nipples hard as he continued plowing into her. It sent her over the edge, her body convulsing wildly as she exploded on the inside. She was flailing so hard that I let go of her arms. She moved her hands to her chest, grabbing her own tits violently as she continued to climax.

Damian stopped fucking her. He stood and tucked his hard cock back into his pants. "Let's go," he said to me.

I didn't want to leave Jennifer lying in the pile of leaves alone although she was in her own world, clearly unaware of her surroundings.

Damian must have sensed my hesitation. He grabbed my hand and pulled me back to the parking lot, which was less than 30 feet away. He knocked on the window and Eric immediately climbed out of his car. "Follow me," Damian ordered Eric.

I leaned against Tawny's car to catch my breath. Dang, what a coup. We rocked that! Damian and I pulled that off without any issues, even with changing the plan and leaving the parking area. I should have felt a greater sense of accomplishment but Damian's proximity continued to throw me off and muddle my emotions.

Damian was back within seconds. "They're good. Let's go," he said.

I followed him back to the building and to my office, not speaking until my door was closed behind us. "Good work," I said.

"Great teamwork," he replied, raising his hand for a high five. I ignored it - I wasn't a ten-year-old.

"Yes, we did well," I said. "I think Jennifer was satisfied."

Damian bent over laughing. "Satisfied? She was a hell of a lot more than satisfied."

Damian was such a cocky bastard. He made my blood boil sometimes. "I'm beat," I said. "I'm going home." I felt an overwhelming need to get out of his orbit.

Damian took the hint. He stood and headed for the door. "I'll stop and see you tomorrow and you can tell me what you think of my idea." I knew he meant us going on a date.

Thankfully he left before I had to come up with a reply. I snatched up my purse and car keys and hustled to the parking lot. As I walked to my Subaru, I noticed Eric's car was gone. I made a mental note to call Jennifer the next day to check on how she was doing.

I collapsed into bed the moment I was home, emotionally and physically exhausted. But sleep didn't come easy. When it did arrive, it was tortured, filled with images of Damian fucking other women.

#####

Saturday was my busiest day of the week. It was always overloaded with bookings and the building itself was often filled to capacity. That was saying a lot considering the size of the building.

I started the workday with a call to Jennifer. She raved for ten minutes straight about how much fun she had the night before. Damian and I had hit a home run with that one.

I was on the phone with a regular when Damian knocked on my door in the early afternoon. I motioned for him to come inside and take a seat. I wrapped up the call when I said, "That will work fine. We'll see you at 10:30. Again, I'm sorry that we can't accommodate you for a longer length of time tonight, Julia."

"Julia Stanton?" Damian asked as I put the phone down on its cradle.

"The one and only." Julia was another of our private area regulars. A gorgeous socialite in her early 30s, Julia got bored and lonely when her husband left town. On those occasions, she called me, frantically begging for an appointment that same day. That was what I'd just dealt with.

Damian chuckled to himself. "That woman is nothing if not predictable."

I smiled at him. "True. But I really like her. It can't be easy being surrounded by so much money and luxury yet feeling so lonely."

Damian wasn't as sympathetic to her plight as I was, I knew from past conversations about Julia. "Yeah, cry me a river. Or wait, let me find my violin." He mimicked playing the instrument.

"Be nice," I said, only half in jest.

Damian stood, turned his back to me, and spanked his very sexy ass. "Consider me properly chastised."

I ignored him, ripping my eyes away from his delicious behind. "Anyway, I'm not sure you are going to like what I have to say."

"I can handle it. Hit me."

"Julia needs to come in tonight…"

"Of course she does," Damian interrupted.

"We have a packed schedule. The only time slot I could give her was from 10:30 to 11. You are the only one available for that 30 minute window."

"That's fine. Why would you think I wouldn't be okay with that?"

"Well, she wants a threesome - one guy and one girl. All our females are fully booked so I'll have to join you two."

Damian's hand shot in the air in a victory punch as he shouted, "Wahoo! That's the best thing I've heard in years!"

"Years. Wow, that is sad. You need to get out more," I said.

"You're right. I need to get out more. Like on a date with you. But tonight with you is perfect. I've been dying to get my hands on you."

"Hold up. It's not about what you want. It's about Julia."

"I know that but you'll be there, too. What's not to like?" Damian asked.

I knew we could go in circles with this conversation for hours so I redirected it. "Room 4F. 10:30 sharp. Add it to the rest of your schedule for the night."

Damian gave me a half-assed salute. "Yes, ma'am."

"Stop the 'ma'am' shit. I feel too much older than you already." Why did I have to keep reminding him of that?

"Yes, Amanda." The smirk on Damian's face was half adorable, half infuriating.

"Any details I need to know before going in the room with Julia?" I asked; I knew from previous bookings that Damian frequently serviced the blonde.

"As I mentioned, she is predictable. She likes the same thing every time. She likes to eat a pussy as she gets fucked from behind by a hard dick. I don't have to spell it out whose role is whose, do I?"

"No, you most certainly do not," I replied.

I glanced at the clock on my wall. "You'd better get going," I said. "Your first appointment will be here soon."

"Yes." Damian stood and headed for the door. "I'll see you this evening," he said.

"10:30. 4F."

"I'll be there. I'm looking forward to it," Damian said, sounding like he meant it more than he should.

"Me, too," I replied, although it pained me to admit it for some reason.

Before I could stop him, Damian came to where I sat, kissed me on the cheek, and raced out of the room before I had a chance to throw another pencil at him.

#####

Nerves had me at 4F ten minutes too early. I fluffed everything in the room, managing to kill a full 30 seconds. Dang, what was I thinking agreeing to this. I was anxious when I was in the same room as Damian these days. Being on the same bed as him would be torturous. This was a first for Damian and me, working on an appointment together. The time in the parking lot with Jennifer had been the only exception, although I hadn't been sexually involved in that scenario.

I lay down on the bed and looked up at myself in the mirror that hung on the ceiling. I thought I looked good. Big hair, make-up that accentuated my green eyes and strong cheekbones. My outfit bordered on boring - a pink teddy that cupped my boobs like a pair of hands and lifted them higher than they were naturally. I'd skipped panties as they'd be off before anything started, if what Damian said turned out to be true.

I hadn't heard anyone enter the room so when a hand touched my thigh, I jumped. I looked over to see Damian with his hands in the air. "Sorry," he said. "I didn't realize you were off in space."

He flopped onto the bed beside me, interlacing his fingers behind his head as he looked at us in the mirror. I discreetly tried to pull the hem of my teddy down to fully cover my crotch. I knew it was an absurd gesture since Damian was probably about to get a full pussy shot when Julia arrived. He was gracious enough not to comment on my nervous fidgeting.

Still looking in the mirror, Damian said, "Hey, we are a good looking couple."

I looked at him, our eyes making contact in the mirror. He continued, "We are such a good looking couple that we should go on a date. What do you think?"

"Really? You are discussing this now, when I am feeling so edgy that I can't stand being in my own skin?"

Damian turned onto his side so he was facing me. He stroked my cheek with a touch so light that I had to press my face into his hand to feel it. "Nice," I purred, the word slipping out without me noticing until it hit my ears.

"You really need to give us a chance," Damian said. "One date. That's it."

"I'm thinking about it," I replied.

"I'm trying to be patient and not rush you."

"I know and I appreciate that."

"I hope so. I'm not known for my patience but you are worth it."

"Damian, I..." The rest of my sentence died before it crossed my lips as our hostess, Angie, entered the room with Julia. Damian jumped to attention, crossing to where Julia stood by the door and bringing her into the room.

"Thank you, Angie," I said. Angie left, closing the door behind her.

We only had 30 minutes to satisfy Julia and Damian didn't waste any time. He nodded at me to move up to the pillows as he picked Julia up and spun her around. Julia squealed like a pig, a sound that turned from ear-piercing to lusty as Damian dropped her on the bed. She looked over at me, her eyes skimming over my body and turning dark. She pushed my legs apart and without asking or hesitating, her face dove into my pussy. Dang, there was no warm up with Julia, which was probably a good thing with the ticking clock looming over us.

Julia ate me out with gusto. I grabbed onto the rails on the headboard to hold myself steady. I looked over at Damian. He was smiling widely at me and when our gazes met, he threw me a thumbs-up sign. "What the fuck?" I mouthed silently, pointing down at Julia's head in my crotch.

"I told you so," he mouthed back.

Damian moved onto the bed between Julia's parted legs. Julia was wearing a dress with a zipper than ran the entire length down the back. He unzipped it from her neck to the hem by her knees and yanked it off. All Julia had on underneath was a garter belt and stockings. No bra, no panties. Holy crap! Julia was a steaming heap of sexiness with her flawless skin and her perfect ass.

Looking at me, Damian slapped Julia's ass hard. I suffered for that as Julia bit down on one of my pussy lips. "Ouch," I said through clenched teeth.

I think Julia mumbled an apology but she was so deep in my core that I couldn't decipher anything she said.

Damian slapped Julia's other ass cheek. She bit down again and I threw Damian a nasty look. I liked my pussy lips attached to my body.

He mouthed, "Sorry," although we both knew he wasn't. With his juvenile attitude, he no doubt thought it was funny.

While still staring at me, Damian grabbed Julia's hips and hoisted her ass a little higher into the air. He used one hand to hold her hips in place while his other hand disappeared between her legs. I could feel Julia moving as Damian rubbed her core.

Damian had only been wearing boxers when he came into the room. He shuffled them down his hips and plowed into Julia. He fucked her as relentlessly as Julia was eating me out, with almost too much enthusiasm. My pussy was flooding with juices - the entire situation was one hell of a turn-on - but Julia was lapping my juice away as soon as it hit. She wasn't a memorable pussy eater but that's because she was doing it for her pleasure, not mine. That worked for me as she was the client.

Julia's orgasm hit without warning. She pulled her face out of my core to scream, gulping in deep breaths once her scream was only an echo in the room. I saw Damian look over at the clock. We still had ten minutes. He said, "Let's see if we can give you another one of those, Julia."

Damian flipped Julia over, her head now between my thighs as she looked up at me. "Hi," she said.

Damian slid back into Julia, his massive cock disappearing into her depths. He bent over her so his face was inches from hers. He proceeded to lick the wet spots off her lips and chin. When he had every drop, he looked up at me as he spoke to Julia, "Amanda tastes great, doesn't she?"

Julia nodded. "Yes. I want more."

Damian motioned for me to oblige as he continued fucking her. I moved onto my knees and squatted over Julia's face, lowering myself enough so her tongue and lips could reach me. It was a great quad workout.

Damian stared at me the entire time he fucked Julia. It was a surreal experience. Damian hadn't touched me since he'd brushed my cheek when it was only the two of us in the room, yet I felt like we were sharing an intimate moment.

One of Damian's hands slid from Julia's tits to her clit. He rubbed at her bud as he kept driving into her. The guy knew how to touch a woman so she would cum, that was obvious. And it was also a major plus as we had a schedule to keep.

With three minutes to spare, Julia cupped my ass cheeks and pushed me up, freeing her face so she could breathe as she climaxed again. The second one hit her harder than the first had. She turned a slight shade of blue as she gasped for air.

Damian held himself still, his shaft still hidden inside Julia. When we had one minute left, Damian pulled out and leaned down to kiss Julia on the cheek. "Have a good night," he said. "It was a pleasure, as always."

Julia mumbled something neither Damian nor I could understand as we headed for the door. I straightened my teddy as Damian tucked his cock into his boxers, the head sticking out of the top. We left the room and Angie entered; it would be her job to get Julia decent and out of the private area.

"Where are you off to next?" I asked Damian; I knew he was booked for another appointment at 11, which it was now.

"Three doors down. Hey, about our date, how does tomorrow night work for you?"

Ignoring his question, I said, "Get to work."

We stopped outside of the door that Damian needed to go into. He glanced at me for a brief second, a look of longing on his face that hit me in a place deep inside. Without a word, he turned from me and went to work. I leaned back against the wall and rested until I didn't feel like I'd been struck by a lightning bolt. Only then did I go back to my office.

Once there, I shed the teddy and stepped into my shower, wanting to wash the feel of Julia's tongue off me. Running the soap over my skin, I clued in that the whole situation with Damian left me more aroused than I'd been in a long time. Sure, I'm often horny but aroused was a whole other thing. I sat on the shower bench, my hand sliding between my legs. My body was wet from the shower but my core was soaked with thick pussy juice. I slid two fingers into my depths, fucking myself as I thought of Damian's hard cock. His shaft was so big that I knew my body would have to stretch to accommodate him. I wondered if he would ever be inside me. I wasn't sure if I wanted that or not. Being aroused by someone wasn't the same as wanting a relationship with that person. Seeing what went on at the club every night drove that point home often.

My other hand moved to rub my clit. I was suddenly desperate to cum, knowing that would allow me to move on from tonight's experience.

I kept playing with my body until I climaxed. It was a doozy and I dragged it out as long as I could, savoring every nuance.

Damn Damian, this was all his fault. Not only had he been working me up the past few days, I'd had to endure fantasizing about being screwed by him as I'd played with myself.

I rinsed my tender pussy extra well before getting out of the shower. Once dressed, I did the rounds of the club, making sure that everything was running smoothly. Other than a lost earring and one whiny lady complaining that she only had four orgasms but wanted five, we had another flawless night.

#####

The club was open seven days a week - there were no days of rest in the sex industry - and I spent the day attacking paperwork and taking calls. I kept expecting Damian to pop by and harass me about going out with him but he never showed. It was his loss as I'd finally made a decision: I was going to put Damian out of his misery and go on one date with him.

My manager, Barbara, and I had a meeting in the late afternoon about the week ahead. When we wrapped up, I decided to head home. It was only six but I was exhausted and ready to curl up on the couch and zone out with a Matthew McConaughey flick.

I grabbed my bag, informed Barbara that she was in charge, and headed for the parking lot. I'd almost reached my

Subaru when someone behind me yelled, "I'll get your door for you."

I turned to see Damian half-running toward me. "Hi," I said, happier than I should have been to see him.

"Hi, Amanda. How are you?"

"Really good. How are you?"

"I'm good, too." He reached around me for my door handle. I stepped to the side so he could pull it open. I tossed my purse onto the passenger seat and turned to face Damian. He stood on the other side of my door, his hands resting on the top to keep the door open.

"Thanks," I said.

"No problem."

I was waiting for him to bring up his date suggestion but he didn't. Disappointment hit me like a punch to the gut. The silence stretched out between us, not uncomfortable.

I slid into my seat so I could look away from Damian; I didn't want him to see anything on my face.

After hesitating for a few seconds in case Damian wanted to say or do something - he didn't - I pulled my legs into my car. Damian closed my door, the sound of the soft slam loud in the stillness of the night. He knocked on the top of my car and said, "Have a good night."

"Yeah. You, too," I replied. Dang, that sounded lame.

I started my car but I didn't put it into drive. I looked up at Damian, silently begging him to ask me about the date. But he didn't. Instead, he just looked down at me with a goofy, sexy grin on his face.

With one last knock on my roof, Damian turned and walked toward the door to the club. As he reached for the door handle, he turned and looked back at me one more time.

"Hey," I yelled. "What about our date?"

"When do you want to do it?"

Right that moment would've worked for me but I knew he was fully booked for the evening. "Tomorrow night?" I suggested.

"Sure. I gotta go. Text me your address and the pick-up time."

"Will do."

Damian flashed me a sexy smile before he disappeared into the club.

I managed to watch *Ghosts of Girlfriends Past* and make it halfway through *Fool's Gold* before I texted Damian. *It's Amanda. How does 8 work for you tomorrow?*

Damian texted me back 45 minutes later. *That works. Address?*

I texted it to him.

*Great. C U tom at 8*

I wasn't ready to end our communication yet. *What are you doing now?* I texted.

*Sure U want 2 know?*

*Yes*

*Jerking off*

Whoa - that wasn't the answer I was expecting. *Didn't you get off at work?*

*No. I rarely cum at work. I stay hard for work & jerk it at home*

Fascinating. I questioned whether it would be rude to ask him why. Then again, he brought it up. *Why not get off at work?*

*Don't feel it. Wd rather cum alone or w/ someone I care about*

*Don't you get blue balls going for hours without release?*

*Nah, used 2 it after all these yrs*

I'm not sure why but I found that to be a total turn-on. Damian was a man of many layers.

Damian texted again a few minutes later: *Any requests 4 date night activities?*

*I'm easy. Anything you plan will be great, I'm sure.*

*Just so you know - I'm not easy. I don't hv sex on the 1st date*

I laughed. Of course he didn't! Damian wouldn't like to be thought of as predictable. *Thanks for the heads up.*

*We need to keep yr expectations realistic*

*Duly noted.*

*Sleep tight, Amanda. C U tom* he texted, ending the chat.

I felt oddly unfulfilled at the abruptly ended conversation. I tried to refocus on Matthew's plight in the movie but I didn't have much luck. My thoughts were too centered on Damian.

#####

I spent the following day at work - as usual - but the hours dragged on like they never had before. All I could think about was my date with Damian that night. It was strange having something on my mind that didn't have to do with work. At six I gave up trying to focus on spreadsheets and headed home to get ready for my date.

By the time my doorman announced Damian's arrival at eight sharp, I was so riddled with nerves that I wanted to vomit. I told the doorman I'd be right down and after a quick glance in the mirror, I grabbed my purse and headed to the elevator.

I crossed the lobby to where Damian stood chatting with my doorman. My mouth fell open. Damian was wearing a tailored suit with all the right accoutrements: smart tie, starched shirt, cuff links that reflected the lobby light, and sleek patent leather shoes. I had a major thing for men that wore patent leather shoes.

I was less than a foot from Damian when he realized I was there. He turned my direction and his eyes widened in a way that made it clear that he liked what he saw. "Amanda, you look beautiful," he said, bending down to kiss my cheek. I'd opted for the classic little black dress and with Damian looking so dashing, I was glad I did.

The doorman wished us a fun night and after thanking him, Damian and I headed outside. "Nice car," I said as he opened the passenger door of an Audi R8.

"Thanks. I'm fond of Betsy myself."

"Where are we going?" I asked as Damian slid the car into first gear and took off.

"Dinner first. I hope you like Italian."

"I love it."

We made small talk as Damian drove and our conversation morphed onto politics and religion as we shared bowls of chickpea soup and spaghetti carbonara. I hadn't been on a date in years. Being out with a handsome, polished man like Damian was refreshing. We never struggled to keep the conversation going and Damian was attentive and proper. But by the time we left the restaurant, one thing was clear: Damian was every woman's wet dream and I could never be in a relationship with him. I wasn't a jealous person but I knew being with Damian would be intolerable. Women were throwing themselves at him, even with me sitting across the table from him. On the way back from the ladies room, I saw the waitress slip Damian a piece of paper, no doubt her number.

When we left the restaurant and went to a club or an after dinner drink, it got worse. Women were even more open about wanting a piece of Damian. He never encouraged it and he was overly attentive to me. But if I'd been his girlfriend, it would have been more than I could handle.

When Damian dropped me off, he asked, "Can I come up?"

I looked over at him, torn between wanting him to ravage my body and wanting him as far from me as possible. "Damian, I had a really nice time tonight. I really did. You are a great guy and fun to be with. Any woman would be lucky to have you. But that woman isn't me."

Damian's face registered surprise and nothing else. He was speechless for many long seconds but finally spoke. "Really? Are you punking me right now? I thought we had a connection tonight."

Dang, how do I even begin to explain this? I knew that no matter what I said, Damian wouldn't fully understand where I was coming from. "We did have a connection. And I had a great time tonight, thank you for that. I just don't see us going anywhere."

"Is it our age difference? That shouldn't matter."

It wasn't that. It was my neurotic issues but I didn't want to divulge that to Damian. I've always had a hard time admitting my shortcomings so I used my fallback excuse. "I don't want to date a colleague. I don't want to ruin our friendship."

"Friendship? You call this a friendship? Every time I look at you, I want to either jump your bones or eat you out until you scream my name. That isn't friendship!"

His words flattered me but I didn't let it show. I shot him down one final time. "That's how it's going to be, Damian. I'm sorry that you aren't happy with my decision but it's not open for discussion."

He didn't seem to know what to say. I took the opportunity to grab the door handle and get out. The slamming door seemed to snap Damian into action, his manners ingrained. He ran to catch up with me, walking me to the door of my building. He kissed my cheek and I walked inside without another word exchanged.

As I watched him walk back to his car, a part of me wanted to run back to Damian, screaming out that I'd made a mistake. Instead, I let him go.

Back in my apartment, I changed into shorts and a t-shirt and crawled into bed. I'd made the right decision about Damian, I just had to wait for my heart to catch up with my head.

Despite being emotionally wiped out, I couldn't sleep. I flipped on the tube, mindlessly watching late night talk shows. Ironically, Matthew McConaughey was on Jimmy Kimmel but I couldn't focus on anything he said. I was debating turning off the TV and cracking open the latest Tilly

Bagshawe book when my phone buzzed. It was a text from Damian. *U still up?*

Did I want to answer him? Or should I ignore it, claiming I'd been asleep if he asked the next time I saw him? I couldn't deny that a part of me missed him, as absurd as that was. I decided to answer him.

As I typed my reply, I steeled myself to stay firm in my decision. *I'm still up.*

*Good. Is there anything I can say or do to change yr mind?*

*I don't mean to sound heartless but no.*

*In that case, can we do 1 thing b4 I accept yr kiss-off?*

*What's that?* A bout of excited dread hit me - I wasn't sure I wanted to hear Damian's answer to my question.

*U've devoted yr life 2 satisfying other peoples fantasies. I want 2 satisfy yrs, whatevr it is. Wd U let me do that?*

I burst into tears. I didn't even know why I was crying. His gesture hit me in a spot deep within myself where I rarely ventured. It was probably a selfish offer on his part as he'd likely get to have his way with me but I was touched nonetheless.

When many minutes passed without me answering - I was still debating what to say - Damian texted: *What is yr ultimate fantasy?*

That was almost embarrassing to admit but somehow the distance offered by texting made it easier to make confessions. *It's such a cliché but me and 2 guys at the same time.*

*Its not a cliché. Its 1 of the most popular fantasies for a reason. Women luv it*

Damian was always letting me off the hook. *True.*

*How does tom nite work 4 U?*

*For what?*

*Making yr fantasy cum true*

My schedule was clear but did I want it to happen? Until that moment, I hadn't realized how much I wanted Damian to have his way with me, if only once. *Sounds good.*

*My place. 10 p.m.* He texted me his address.

*See you tomorrow.*
*Looking 4ward 2 it*
*Me too*

I tossed my phone on my nightstand and turned off the TV. Great. Thanks to Damian I would never get to sleep tonight. How could I when thoughts of tomorrow night wouldn't stop racing through my mind. Who would the other guy be? Would Damian be as great of a lover as I imagined him to be? How many times would I get off? Would I have so much fun that I'd buckle under the weight of it? I had so much to look forward to!

#####

I was ten minutes late getting to Damian's place. I didn't mean to be; Google Maps threw me off and sent me down a few wrong roads. By the time I pulled into the driveway of a typical two-storey house in the suburbs, I was frazzled. I hated being late.

I had on a white blouse and a pencil skirt as I had no idea what one wore to a three-way. I found my hands smoothing the sides of the skirt down as I approached the front door. Or maybe my hands were trying to wipe the dampness from my palms…

When I reached the door, I spotted a yellow sticky note at eye level. *Come on it* it read. I turned the knob and stepped inside. Only a few lamps were on but there was enough light to see a line of rose petals leading through the house. I closed the door behind me and followed the flower trail through a living room filled with oversized furniture and continuing up a set of stairs. I climbed the steps to the second floor, still following the petals.

All the doors were shut but the flower trail stopped clearly outside of the door at the furthest end of the hall. Taking a deep breath, I walked to the designated door and I took a moment to calm myself before I knocked.

I didn't have the chance to knock. The door handle turned and the door swung inward a couple of inches. I took the hint and pushed the door open further, slowly stepping into the room. It was massive bedroom. A California king-sized bed flanked by nightstands was the only furniture in the space. Over a dozen candles sat on shelves scattered around the room, providing plenty of illumination. Damian stood by the bed and when our eyes connected, he walked to where I stood; his smile grew bigger the closer he got to me. "Amanda, it's great to see you. I'm glad you came."

"You are too hot to resist," I said, playfully swatting his hard chest.

Damian cupped my face with his hands, his thumbs caressing my jaw as his fingers dug into the back of my neck. He bent down and kissed my cheek as he said, "Hold still. Don't flinch."

I had no idea what was about to happen so I took a deep breath to stay calm. I felt more than saw someone approach me from behind. Whoever it was raised their hands above my head and a sash moved in front of my face. As the stranger behind me adjusted the material so it covered my eyes, I said, "I prefer to watch. Can you leave that off?"

"We'll take it off in a bit," Damian replied.

I let out a sigh of disappointment but Damian didn't relent. The sash was knotted tightly behind my head, the material fully covering my eyes. Damian's thumbs tapped down the material in the front so it lay flat against my cheeks.

Damian's lips connected with mine as his tongue gently pushed its way into my mouth. It hit me that it's been a long time since I'd been kissed. I mean really kissed by someone who meant it. I parted my lips and let his tongue into my mouth, our tongues softly sparring as Damian's hands continued to firmly hold my head.

Hands wrapped around my waist from behind and slowly worked their way up to my collarbone. A hand traced the collar of my blouse before zeroing in on the buttons.

Starting at the top one, whoever was behind me undid them one at a time. When whom I assumed was a guy reached my waist, he tugged my blouse out of my skirt and continued undoing the buttons. When he reached the bottom, he slid my top down my arms, leaving me in only my bra, skirt, and panties. The stranger rubbed my arms and shoulders before slowly moving onto my back. During the rubdown, Damian continued kissing me, his lips and tongue doing a thorough job of exploring every crevice in my mouth. Damian sure knew how to kiss a woman and make her feel like she was the most desirable person in the world.

My bra snapped undone. Fingers trailed up my back and onto my shoulders, slipping under my bra straps to push them down my arms. The bra fell free from my body. The relief of my boobs no longer being restrained was palpable. A moan escaped from my throat, muffled between my mouth and Damian's. Damian still hadn't let up on my jaw and his caressing touch on my face was a major aphrodisiac.

The person behind me was definitely a man; he moved closer to me and a hard cock pressed into my butt cheek. His hands moved from my arms and circled around to my front, gently cupping my breasts. The soft exploring quickly turned firmer as the intensity of his touch turned heated. My nipples grew harder until they were aching, my arousal level increasing with every erotic touch.

I was having trouble catching my breath. I didn't want to but I pulled away from Damian's luscious lips. I gulped in lungfuls of air. The hands playing with my tits grew rough and I desperately wanted someone's mouth on my nipples. "Suck my nipples," I said just loud enough for Damian to hear.

I couldn't see Damian but I felt him lower his body onto his knees. Taking a boob in each of his hands, his mouth made love to my tits. Not surprising, he knew how to touch boobs so a bolt of lust shot from my nipples to my crotch. I could feel myself growing wetter by the second. It wouldn't be long before my pussy was dripping, leaving a puddle on the floor between my legs.

The guy behind me moved his hands down to my skirt. He slid open the zipper on the side and worked the skirt down over my hips. It fell to the floor, pooling around my ankles. That left me in nothing but a thong.

Damian was still working on my tits and the other two hands were molding my ass, squeezing and rubbing my cheeks. Occasionally he'd spank my ass, not hard enough to sting but hard enough to make a sound that echoed around the room.

I raised my arms, digging my hands into my hair as if I was in the throes of sexual euphoria. But I was actually subtly working the sash a tad bit higher so I could peek out of the bottom. Neither of the guys must've noticed as no one stopped me. I was able to manoeuvre the material up enough so I could see a sliver out of the bottom. It was just far enough to see Damian kneeling in front of me. The sight of my nipples disappearing into his mouth caused my pussy to flood.

The hands on my ass moved around to the front of my thighs, kneading the thick flesh before moving upward. When he cupped my mound, a finger sliding around my pussy lips over my thong, my knees buckled; I hadn't realized how worked up I was. Before I collapsed, the guy behind me swooped me up in his arms and tossed me in the air. I let out a scream as the action was so unexpected.

I landed on the bed, rolling over onto my front as momentum took over me. I moved to roll onto my back so I could watch the action but a pair of hands stopped me, pinning me face down on the bed. Having the blindfold up enough to see a sliver out of the bottom didn't help when my face was shoved into a pillow.

Hands stayed on my back as someone moved between my legs from behind. My thighs were shoved apart and my thong was ripped off. The tearing noise was one of the most erotic sounds I had ever heard. Someone settled between my thighs. Fingers moved into my naked core and began a slow exploration of my pussy area. Fingers did laps around my pussy lips and tickled at my clit from time to time. It resulted in a slow build up to what I knew would be a knockout orgasm, one I equated to a home run in baseball. I didn't fight it. I let the orgasm keep building as time flowed slowly by. I figured we weren't on a time schedule so I did nothing but lay there and take it, lapping up every delicious touch and spasm.

By the time I came, I felt like my clit was swollen to the size of a manhole cover. I was going out of my mind with lust. The orgasm was a knockout as I knew it would be. It left me wiped out in the best ways, my sexual satisfaction at an all-time high. Men who knew how to make a woman cum without sliding anything - including themselves - into her were a rare breed.

When I had gathered enough strength to move my arms, I raised a hand to my head and yanked off the blindfold; I didn't care if the guys got mad, I wanted to see every moment of the rest of the night. It took a few blinks for my eyes to adjust to the brightness even though it was only candlelight.

Neither of the men noticed that I could now see as they were too busy rigging a swing of some sort to the ceiling. Both of the men were naked and had hard-ons. Both were smokin' hot. Damian's sex appeal was a given but his friend was equally incredible. He looked like he was from Greece, glistening olive skin and a body chiselled from human granite. I couldn't wait to be the filling in that stud sandwich!

Damian glanced over at me and smiled. My heart melted even as my crotch throbbed, already ready for more. He left the swing to his buddy and came to the bed. He grabbed my ankle and yanked me to the end of the bed, close to him. He took a firm grip on my waist and hoisted me up and onto his shoulder. What was with these men wanting to carry women? Whatever it was, I loved it. Another bonus was the view I had of Damian's ass just below my head. I reached down and took one of his butt cheeks in each of my hands, squeezing them hard. Damian responded by slapping my ass hard, his other hand holding me steady on his shoulder. When I tensed up, he slapped my ass a second time, his fingernails digging into the meat of my butt. The pain was a turn-on, another in a long line of turn-ons I'd been exposed to since I arrived at Damian's house.

I screamed as Damian bucked and threw me off his shoulder. I landed in the swing, my butt in the dipped part made for rear ends; Damian had perfect aim. That wasn't surprising as every part of him was perfect.

My legs spread apart as my ankles were hooked into stirrups. Damian and the other hottie stood between my feet, both looking at me intensely, their cocks pointing my direction. Damian said, "Amanda, this is Ricky. Ricky, Amanda."

"Hi, Ricky," I said, my breath coming out in a gasp as the sight in front of me was every woman's wet dream. I was already soaking wet.

"Who do you want to fuck you first?" Damian asked me.

That was an impossible question to answer. "Surprise me," I said.

Damian and Ricky looked at each other. Damian shrugged, a slight movement that I barely noticed. Ricky playfully pushed Damian to the side, moved so he was centered between my legs, grabbed a pair of handles on the swing, and drove into me.

Dang, Ricky filled me up, my body working to stretch around him. My eyes rolled into the back of my head as he plunged into me over and over again, the swing the only thing keeping my body from sling-shotting across the room.

Ricky barely got into the groove of fucking me when Damian pushed him aside and took his spot between my legs. Instead of grabbing the handles, he took a firm grip on the tops of my thighs and plunged into me. Holy crap! I felt like

I'd been nailed by a tire iron. Damian was on a roll when Ricky nudged him aside. "My turn. I want another piece."

I closed my eyes and rested my head back, resigned to my blissful sexual romp in the swing. I was the happiest woman in the world at that moment and I took in every nuance.

Ricky and Damian were very different lovers. They had cocks that were the same size when hard but they worked them in opposing ways. Neither was better than the other, although I was a tad partial to Damian being inside me as I was also attracted to his personality. I didn't know Ricky at all. Then again, the allure of sex with a total stranger was undeniable and the only thing I knew about Ricky was his name and that he looked like a human lollipop.

The two men continued plundering me, one guy, then the other, and back again. My body flourished with every thrust. Another orgasm started brewing and I let it creep up at its own speed, not rushing or slowing down its arrival. By the time it hit with the power of a landslide, my body had long since turned gelatinous.

I screamed as I climaxed, although I didn't register what I'd mumbled. Whoever was fucking me slowed his pace to turtle speed as my pussy contracted wildly.

I took my time returning to reality, preferring to languish in the aftershocks of my orgasm. When I finally cracked an eye open, Ricky was smiling at me, a wicked look on his face. A rash of goose bumps covered my body as a realization hit me - as glorious as the night had been to that point, the best was yet to come.

Ricky slowly slid out of me as he continued leering. He reached out a hand to me and I took it. He gently pulled me out of the swing and held me around my waist until the blood flowed back into my legs and I could stand on my own. Taking my hand again, he led me back to the bed where the most spectacular sight lay in front of me: Damian was lying on his back, his hands behind his head, his cock pointing up at the ceiling. A fresh wave of lust hit me as I looked at Damian sprawled out on the bed. I doubted I would ever find another guy as sexy as he was.

I climbed onto the bed on all fours, stopping when my face was level with his crotch. I bent down and took just the head of his cock into my mouth. I sealed my lips tight around the ridge that circled the head of his dick as my tongue rubbed and flicked him. "Oh, Amanda," Damian moaned. "Yeah, baby, that's good…."

The head of his cock fully played with, I slowly slid my lips all the way down the length of his shaft. Damian's legs tensed up as he buried a hand in my hair. "Yeah," he moaned again.

As I stroked him with my mouth, I tasted myself on him. Thinking of him being deep inside me was a major turn-on. Just the image of it caused my speed to double, my mouth pumping up and down his shaft with gusto.

I felt Ricky move behind me. He nudged my legs apart as he settled between my thighs. His cock was poking my butt cheek as his hands roamed over my rear. "You have a great ass, Amanda," Ricky said. All those years of Pilates have been worth it.

One of Ricky's hands slid from my ass to my pussy. He played with my core, moving his fingers around my pussy lips and over my sensitive clit. He spanked my ass with this cock and it felt like I was being hit with a two by four.

I was still mouth fucking Damian when Ricky spread my butt cheeks apart and drove his cock into my pussy. In the first few seconds, I knew it would be hard to continue the blowjob when Ricky was driving into me so hard that my body wouldn't stop moving.

After leaving as much saliva on Damian's dick as I could, I pulled my face off him and started stroking his cock with my hand. My other hand rested on the bed, trying to keep myself as steady as I could; that wasn't easy considering how enthusiastically Ricky was fucking me from behind. And

Ricky felt so amazing that I was tempted to flop down on the bed beside Damian and let Ricky ravage me. The only thing that stopped me from doing that was wanting to watch Damian shoot his load. Ever since he'd admitted that he typically came at home alone instead of at the club with others, seeing him blow has been a goal of mine.

Ignoring the slow burn that was starting to build in my pumping arm, I kept up my stroking speed, adding more saliva onto Damian's shaft when needed. We continued like that for many long, delicious minutes - Ricky fucking me as I played with Damian's cock like he was an instrument and I was a concert-level musician.

When Damian's entire body started to tense up, I figured he was close to blowing. I soaked his cock with a fresh batch of saliva and picked up my pumping speed a fraction more. Sure enough, less than 30 seconds later, Damian hissed, "Slow it up, Amanda."

I did as he asked and reduced my pumping rate by 75%. His cock exploded, streams of jism shooting all over the place. Some ended up in my hair, a few droplets on my cheek. A caterpillar-sized dribble landed on my left boob. More oozed out of him as I continued slowly stroking his shaft.

When he was emptied out, Damian peeled my hand off his cock and slowly rolled to the side of the bed. Ricky took the opportunity to switch positions, flipping me over, hoisting my feet onto his shoulders, and driving into me from the front. He kept one hand on my thigh to keep my legs from flailing to the side. His other hand moved to my clit, gently rubbing and tickling the nub. Between Ricky's cock hitting my g-spot occasionally and his persistent clit massaging, the orgasm that had been slowly building at the speed of a sloth now came at me like a speeding truck. My body tensed, preparing for the tsunami that was about to hit.

Ricky was still driving into me when I came, my entire body wracked with spasms. I loved how every orgasm was just a little different from the others and that one hit me extra deep inside. My core was on fire in all the best ways.

I startled out of my self-indulgent post-orgasm haze when Ricky abruptly let go of my thigh and pulled back a few inches. He took a firm hold on his cock and stroked himself, the head of his cock pointing my direction.

I got off on watching men play with themselves. I was mesmerized by Ricky's near frantic jerking motions. When he suddenly stopped, I held my breath, anticipating being shot by his jism. As I'd figured, a second later he erupted, his cum spraying all over me. I ran my fingers through a puddle that was pooling in the valley between my tits. His warm cum was slick on my nipples.

Ricky gave my ass a gentle slap as he lowered my legs to the bed. "You rock, Amanda," he said as he stepped away from me.

"You're not so bad yourself," I said to Ricky. "It was great to meet you."

With one last clench on my thigh, he said, "You, too."

Damian came at me from the side, still naked. No matter how often I saw him nude, he continued to astonish me.

He picked me up and slung me over his shoulder in a fireman's carry. I didn't resist although I doubted I could have as I was still reeling from my own climax.

We left the room and Damian carried me to another room down the hall. It was a bedroom with an attached bathroom. He dropped me into a claw-footed bathtub that was full of warm water. Water sloshed over the sides but Damian didn't seem to care. He ran his hands over my body as he said, "Let's get you cleaned up."

Damian's hands kept roving over my body, his hands sloughing every inch of my skin. He even ran a hand between my legs a couple of times, my sensitive-from-overuse clit shooting bolts of desire through me.

Thirty seconds after he'd plunged me into the tub, Damian plucked me out and stood me on the bathmat. He snatched a towel off a hook on the wall and ran it over my body. When I was dry enough, Damian swooped me into his arms and carried me out of the bathroom. He dropped me onto the side of the bed that the duvet had been pulled back from. As I stretched like a cat, my limbs heavy with laziness after the night's events, Damian covered me with the duvet. He carefully tucked it around me and under my chin. I closed my eyes, planning to give in to the exhaustion that was trying to claim my body.

Damian had other plans. The duvet by my feet fluffed up and I felt him slither underneath it. He worked his way up my legs, leaving a trail of kisses up my thigh. His mouth stopped when it reached my core, his tongue lazily exploring my pussy area. His tongue stroked my pussy lips repeatedly, moving them from side to side as his tongue played with every bit of me. I'd never had a guy pay so much attention to my pussy lips; it was heavenly. My body loved it, too. I could feel my juices kicking in although Damian slurped them away as soon as they hit.

When Damian tucked me into bed, I would've bet my last dollar that I had nothing sexually left in me but I was wrong. When Damian's tongue moved from my pussy lips to my clit, a fire sparked to life deep in my core.

I lay there like a mannequin, not moving but embracing every sensation that was taking place inside me. Since I didn't care if I came again - I was more than satisfied - all I did was absorb every touch.

Damian was a master with his tongue, making love to my clit as expertly as his cock had fucked my pussy. An orgasm continued to build as Damian's tongue continued its stroking.

Damian's hands had been resting on the outsides of my hips but one of them crept up my torso to play with my tits. My nipples were on overkill already. Damian seemed to sense that and gently tweaked my nips and rolled them between his fingers with a light touch.

Everything combined, including the thought of Damian between my thighs, led to one of the slowest build-ups to an orgasm that I'd ever had. Because of that, I knew it was going to be an extravaganza I wouldn't easily forget long after I came. Many, many long minutes later with Damian's tongue never letting up on my clit, I climaxed, the orgasm hitting me in one massive wave like a sexual avalanche.

"Holy fuck," I screamed, the sound loud in the room after not having uttered one syllable the entire time Damian had been under the covers. My body seized up, completely drained and overloaded. It was almost too much, in the best possible way. My legs tried to close to stop the stimulation in my core and Damian took the hint, sliding out from under the covers.

My eyes were sealed shut but I felt Damian move near my head as if from down a long tunnel. He kissed my cheek and retucked the duvet securely around me. I wanted to thank him but I didn't have the strength to do even that.

I heard Damian leave the room, the door closing behind him. I succumbed to the bliss and the exhaustion, falling into a coma-like sleep. My last thought before my mind shut off was that I had the greatest life anyone could ever hope for. It didn't get any better than being the owner of a swingers club.

##########

The Swinger's Club: Natalie Smyth

As I straightened my skirt around my hips, I looked down at the man on the bed with disgust. What the hell had I been thinking?

Lonely and horny, I'd driven to a bar across town where no one knew me. After a few drinks to loosen my inhibitions, I'd let a guy pick me up. We went back to his apartment for what I'd hoped would be a night of mutually satisfying sex. Wrong! It turned out to be a three minute dud romp.

He didn't even bother with most of my clothes. He'd snaked a hand under my skirt and ripped off my panties. I hadn't even had a chance to start getting into it when he'd rammed his half-limp dick into me. It hurt as I wasn't wet enough. He blew his load less than a minute later. He'd rolled over and fallen into a deep sleep without uttering a word. His snores felt like sandpaper rubbing my eardrums. I lay beside him on his dirty sheets and fumed. What a jackass! But the real moron had been me for thinking I would find my satisfaction from a guy in a bar. He didn't care about me getting off, only himself. I would've been better off hiring a male prostitute for an hour of pleasure.

I left the dirtbag's apartment and went back to my studio loft to masturbate. That's what I should have done to begin with. I was on the verge of giving up all hope that I would ever find a man who cared about a woman cuming before he did.

#####

The next day at work was a slow one. I spent my first break mentally reliving the frustrating night before. I decided I wasn't ready to give up on the idea of a satisfying sexual experience with a real man, not just my vibrator. Back at my computer, I delved into options for a decent sex partner. I'd figured a male prostitute was the way to go; a guy who got paid to please people for a living should be able to give me an orgasm or two. While searching for one that came highly recommended, some place called The Swinger's Club kept popping up. I clicked on the link and a professional website showed a swanky club for swingers.

Swinging was something I'd never considered before, only because I didn't know much about it. But the more I read about the club, the more I wanted to check it out.

The only clincher for me was that you had to go as a couple. I had no one to take with me. I spent my lunch hour pondering that roadblock and came up with a solution: Danny.

Danny was the payroll guy at the firm where I worked. I knew from conversations that were impossible not to overhear (Danny had a megaphone for a mouth) that he had a pervy sexual side. He'd probably love to accompany me to The Swinger's Club. But I didn't want him to blab to everyone at work that I asked him to be my 'date' to the club.

I remotely logged onto Danny's computer and went searching. I knew what I was doing wasn't allowed but once I found what I was looking for, I was confident Danny wouldn't report me. The guy was into bestiality and was stupid enough to keep an assortment of pictures of himself with animals on his computer. People like Danny were clueless and had no idea how unsecure their private lives were. Especially the stuff they kept on computers and devices.

I printed off two shots of Danny with animals and headed off to find my colleague. I tracked Danny down in the photocopy room. "Hey, Danny," I said, working hard to inject some lightness into my voice.

"Well, if it isn't Natalie. What brings you to this neck of the woods?"

"Do you have a minute to talk? I have an idea I want to run by you."

He looked around the room that was empty except for the two of us. "Right here works," he said.

"I don't want anyone to overhear us. Trust me - you don't either," I said.

"Ooh. Mysterious. I like it." He grabbed a stack of papers from a copier and said, "Follow me."

I trailed behind him as he led me to his office. Damn, Danny had a great butt. His tailored suit helped it look even more squeezable. It was a shame he was such a cocky asshole as he might've made a decent bedroom playmate.

Once in his office, Danny gestured to a chair and said, "Sit down."

I closed his door and took a seat. He took the chair next to it, our feet nearly touching. "What can I help you with?" he asked.

"This is a personal and delicate thing to discuss."

"Shouldn't you be seeing someone in HR instead of me?"

I laughed. "Nope."

Danny stayed quiet, waiting for me to move forward. I took a deep breath and spoke, "I'm just going to spit it out. I need someone to go to a swinger's club with me but I have to take a partner. You came to mind."

I could tell I'd stunned him. He didn't say anything so I continued, "You don't have to do anything with me, not to worry. You and I will go together but we go our separate ways once we find a couple to hook up with. You go off with the woman, me with the guy." After a pause, I asked, "Is that something you would be interested in?"

When he could speak again, he replied, "Hell yeah. I'd be happy to help you out."

Well, that was easy. "Good. Want to check your schedule and see what night works best for you?"

"I don't need to. You pick a day and I'll make it work."

"How about this Friday?" Today was Monday; hopefully he didn't already have plans for the start of the weekend.

"Sure. Friday is great."

"Excellent. Shall we say nine o'clock, if they still have space left in that time slot?"

"Sure."

"Okay. I'll pick you up as you are between my place and the club."

"I can pick you up."

"I prefer to pick you up." I didn't want him anywhere near my personal space. "It makes no sense for you to pick me as you'd be backtracking," I said, throwing out a plausible excuse to cover that I didn't want him to know where I lived.

"Okay, sure. If you insist."

"I do. I'll be at your place at 8:45." I'd already scoped out his address; he lived less than ten minutes from the club.

"I'll be ready. I just have one question," he said.

"What's that?"

"Why me?"

I figured I'd throw him a bone and stroke his ego for being so agreeable to my plan. "Because you are a sexy guy. And I thought this would be right up your alley."

"Well, you are right about that. Thanks for asking me." I could tell it pained him to express gratitude.

"One more thing before I go," I said. I took the two pictures out of the file folder I'd been carrying and handed them to Danny. "I want to make sure we are on the same page. No one at work or anywhere else will hear about this. If they do, posters of those two shots will end up on the walls in the conference room. And in the cafeteria. And they'll be life size shots."

Danny hadn't taken his eyes off the pictures. I could tell he was stunned. "Are you threatening me?" he asked.

"Absolutely not. I'm merely letting you know how this is going to work."

"Where did you get these?"

"That doesn't matter." When Danny didn't say anything, I continued, "So we are on the same page? This stays between us?"

A vein bulged in Danny's neck. I could almost see steam coming out of his ears. "Yes. This is our secret."

"Thank you." I stood and headed for his door. "I'll be at your place at 8:45 Friday," I reiterated.

"I'll be ready."

As I left, I watched Danny slump into his chair, his eyes still glued to the pictures. It couldn't have been easy to get those handed to you. But I had no choice - I had to pull out the heavy artillery to make sure Danny stayed quiet. No way did I want anyone else knowing my business.

######

Once I'd booked Danny and me in the nine p.m. slot Friday and stopped by his office to let him know, I put The Swinger's Club out of my mind. I had an uncanny ability to compartmentalize things in my mind when I wanted to. The rest of Monday and Tuesday passed with me giving it barely a thought. Wednesday I suffered a moment of panic when it hit me that I needed to do more than shower and throw on a pair of jeans and a t-shirt to go to the club. Based on the pictures I saw on their website, the place looked formal.

I stopped at a fancy dress shop on my way home from work and told the saleslady to pick out what she thought looked best on me. I left the store with a simple black dress that hugged me in all the right places. It stopped at my knees so I also picked up a pair of black heels.

Once home, I called and booked an appointment for 6 p.m. Friday at a place that did hair and make-up. I'd used the salon a couple times in the past when I'd had to loose my geek vibe. They could pull off miracles.

Thursday was passing uneventfully when Danny poked his head into my office. He had a piece of scrap paper and a pen in his hand. He passed both to me. "Jot down your phone number," he ordered.

"Good afternoon, Danny. It's nice to see you. How are you?" I asked, sarcasm dripping from my words. One of my pet peeves is people who don't say hello, just barrel into a conversation. Society is losing its sense of civility.

"You've seen me playing with a horse's cock so I don't feel a need for pleasantries. Phone number," he said.

When I didn't make a move for the pen, he put on a fake smile and said, "Please." I could tell saying that word was hard for him. "You'll be glad you did."

It bothered me that I got joy out of making Danny mad or uncomfortable. That wasn't typical of me. I was usually considerate of others and didn't get pleasure when people suffered. I held doors for everyone, took bugs outside instead of squashing them, and took other people's feelings into account. But I didn't do any of those things with Danny and that wasn't right. He was helping me out big time the following day. What he did with animals wasn't my business anyway.

"I'm sorry," I said. "You caught me at a bad moment." It was a lie but I felt better for saying it.

I picked up the pen and jotted my number on the piece of paper. Wanting to lighten the mood, I asked, "Going to send me dick pics?"

"Do you want me to?"

Holy crap - he couldn't tell a joke from a serious question. "As you like," I said, not wanting to crush Danny by giving him a flat out no.

He broke into a laugh. "I'm pulling your leg, Natalie. Don't worry, I won't send you any nudie pics. You should have seen your face when I suggested it!"

So he did have a sense of humor after all. I tossed the pen and paper in his general direction. The pen clattered to the floor. I watched Danny pick it up. Even with a suit on, you could tell he had a firm body and a fine ass. It was such a shame I wasn't attracted to him.

Danny left without saying a word. My phone chimed with a text less than a minute later. *Danny here. This is easier to ask via text than 2 ur face. Why do U want 2 go 2 a swinging club?*

I put my phone down on my desk as I pondered how to reply. Should I tell him the truth? Or keep my reasons private? I decided to go with a light answer: *seems like it would be fun*

*U feeling sexually unsatisfied?*

Ignoring his question, I replied *looking at options, life needs variety*

*OK*

*Y do you ask?*

*If U had an issue with not being sexually satisfied, I hv the solution for U.*

*Okay, I'll bite*

*His name is Park. I've known him since high school. He is apparently the greatest lover in the world. All his g/f raved about him. I could C if he is free 2nite.*

Was he serious? *free for what?*

*U know what I'm talking about. Give me 5 mins, BRB.*

I spun around in my chair and played catch with my hacky sack as I passed the time. When my phone pinged, I reached out for it with more excitement than I should have. *Park said U can swing by his place after 10 2nite.* An address followed seconds later.

*i'll think about it*

*Park said show or no show he'll be there. C U tom nite.*

*k*

As the day passed, I changed my mind a dozen times as to what I was going to do about Park. Going to his place was no different from picking up a guy at the bar and going back to his place. At least with Park there is a greater likelihood that I'd leave his place satisfied, if his past lovers were to be believed.

By eight that night, I made up my mind that I would go. I took a long shower, put on a pair of jeans and a t-shirt, and plugged Park's address into my phone. As I drove to his place in my supped up Honda, I debated if I should take something. I wasn't sure of the protocol for a booty call with someone you had never met before. Figuring a bottle of wine was always welcome, I stopped at a liquor store and picked up my current favorite bottle - Lambrusco.

It was a few minutes before ten when I pulled up in front of a small bungalow that featured an immaculately kept front yard. Danny had said anytime after ten. I didn't want to go to the door before I was supposed to. I was playing on my phone when I heard someone yell, "Hey, Natalie."

I jumped, hitting my hand on my steering wheel. "Ouch," I uttered to myself. Rubbing my sore wrist with my good hand, I looked toward the voice that had yelled my name. Holy shit, had I stepped onto the scene of a Grizzly Adams movie? The guy was standing on his front step and wore a pair of jeans and nothing else. His feet were bare, as was his chest; his very broad well-muscled chest. His shoulders were almost as wide as his front door. His face was half covered by a beard. Piercing jade eyes were filled with humor as he looked at me. His smile reached the sides of his eyes. He was not my usual type but my type wasn't doing it for me lately.

"You okay?" he asked as he started down his steps and walked toward my Honda. I must've said, "Ouch," louder than I thought.

"Yes, fine," I mumbled.

Park reached me and swung my door open. I had no choice but to step out. "You are Park, I'm guessing?"

"Yes I am. And you are the luscious Natalie?"

I half laughed, half snorted, covering my mouth to mask the embarrassing pig noise. "I'm Natalie." Although no one has ever accused me of being luscious before.

I reached back and grabbed the bottle of wine from the car. "I hope you like Lambrusco?" I said.

Park swooped me up into his arms, kicked my car door shut, and carried me up to his house like I weighed nothing. The home we entered was modern and clean; Park has clearly put a lot of work and love into his home. As he dropped me on a massive couch, I said, "Nice place. You are obviously good with your hands."

He leered at me. "You have no idea."

"I meant with your home improvements. You've put…" I gave up, hating when I fumbled over my words.

"I know, Natalie. All good. Wine?" he asked, holding up the bottle I brought.

"Yes. Please." Hopefully the wine would help calm my nerves. Being in Park's presence was throwing me off. He oozed so much charisma that it was intimidating. His naked chest wasn't helping either.

"Let me help you," I said, following him into a chrome and glass kitchen.

Park pointed to a cabinet and said, "Glasses."

I chose two and took them to where Park stood by a counter with the open bottle. I plopped the glasses down and watched in silence as Park filled both glasses almost to the rim. Park picked both of them up and handed one to me. "Cheers," he said. "To a fun-filled night."

We clinked glasses and I took a big gulp, almost choking when too much wine tried to go down my throat at one time. Sputtering, I covered my mouth but a few dribbles escaped my lips. I put my glass down without paying attention and it tipped onto its side, sloshing the red liquid over every inch of the countertop.

Park jumped into action, tossing me a tea towel as he threw another one onto the pool of wine rolling across his counter. I coughed heavily into the towel, finally able to clear my airway and breathe. Park tossed the wine-soaked towel into the sink and started wiping the countertop with a wet dishrag.

Mortified, I folded the towel in my hands into a perfect little square and placed it on the corner of the counter. "I'm going to go. I'm so embarrassed. I'm sorry for the trouble." I had learned long ago to be comfortable with my klutziness but this was more than I could handle.

Tossing the rag in the sink, Park came to where I stood and put a hand on my shoulder. His other hand moved under my chin and tilted my head up so I looked into his face. His eyes were an even deeper shade of green this close. "Nonsense," he said. "You just need to relax. I can help you with that."

Lightly, his hand on my shoulder pushed me back until I ran into the refrigerator. Thankfully he didn't push me too fast or I would've tripped over my own feet, likely whacking my head on the counter as I went down.

"Close your eyes," Park said. I did as he asked. "Take a deep breath." I did that, too. "Another," he said. I obliged, feeling calmer already. "I want you to trust me. Just go with this," Park said.

"Okay." I kept my eyes closed as the sight of Park's hunky self was a big part of why I was off-kilter.

Park's hands cupped my shoulders and ran down my arms, leaving my arms hanging limply at my sides. His hands skipped over to my waist. It felt like he was bunching my t-shirt in a ball around my belly button. I peeked out of one eye and glanced down to see him tying a knot in my shirt so it left my stomach uncovered. For once, I was glad I'd upped my crunches during my workouts.

Park's hands shifted to the waist of my jeans. He dug two fingers into the denim and ran them around my waist, stopping at the button of my jeans. He pulled it through the hole and moved on to the zipper. That undone, my jeans fell loosely away from my body. With his palm resting against my stomach, Park slid his hand down into my panties, not stopping until his hand cupped my mound.

Park's other hand dug into my hair, pinning the back of my head against the fridge. His face burrowed into my neck. His lips made small sucks on my sensitive skin. A rash of goose bumps broke out and covered my body; whether that was from his hands or his lips, I wasn't sure.

"Christ, you are hot down there. Your pussy...," Park said.

I had no idea what to say to that as I wasn't 100% sure that was a compliment. I let the comment hang there unanswered.

Park pulled his hand up a few inches so his fingertips were level with my clit. Moving slowly at first, he rubbed my bud. I could feel the blood flowing to my core, swelling my clit the more Park touched it. He kept his other hand buried in my hair and his lips on my neck as he continued stroking the growing bud.

I felt an orgasm start to build, surprising me as I usually had a hard time cuming when I wasn't completely relaxed. Obviously Park had magic fingers that pulled the tension from my body.

Park was gentle but relentless. My clit felt like it was the size of a bike tire. A few more minutes of rubbing and I would climax with my back digging into his fridge. The whole experience was surreal.

Park's fingers left my clit and moved further south. He slid two fingers around my pussy lips before slipping them into me. They explored my pussy walls, making me jump when he hit a sensitive spot. I'd never felt like that before, like I was getting a pussy massage.

I was just getting into the rhythm of the finger fucking when Park's attention returned to my clit. The orgasm that had been building fell to the wayside even as Park ignited another one. His nibbling on my neck grew more intense as he increased the pressure on my clit.

His fingers were ruthless, never giving my clit a break. Not that she needed one - she was in heaven. It had been years since a man gave me an orgasm induced solely by clit rubbing; my swollen bud was thriving under the attention.

Park was kissing my collarbone when I passed the point of no return. My hands had been hanging limply at my sides but they reared up and grabbed Park's wrist where it stuck out of the top of my jeans, putting a stop to his movements.

"Shit yeah," I screamed, the sound shocking me as I didn't know I'd spoken until it registered in my ears.

The orgasm hit with a wallop. It would've knocked me off my feet had I not been pinned between Park and the fridge. I stood still, enjoying the waves of pleasure that coursed through my body. Rashes of goose bumps broke out where the waves brushed against the underside of my skin. Within seconds, my entire body was covered with the tiny, temporary bumps; that was a clear indication that the orgasm was a memorable one.

Park was the first of us to move. He slowly inched back, making no fast moves until he saw that I could hold myself up. As he stepped away from me to get a new wine glass out of the cabinet, my legs gently buckled; I wasn't as steady as I'd thought. I slowly slid down the fridge, not stopping until my ass connected with the floor. I extended my legs straight out in front of me while my back remained plastered against the fridge.

"You okay?" Park asked, looking at me with a goofy grin as he filled up the new wine glass.

A horrific sound flew from my lips. It was a cross between a hyena's laugh and a witch's cackle. I quickly covered my mouth with my hand to stifle the noise. I took a couple of deep breaths before answering, "I'm great. Thank you." And I meant it - my body felt a million times more relaxed than when I'd pulled up in front of Park's house.

Park handed me a new, filled wine glass and I sipped at the cool drink until every drop was gone. Only then did I make eye contact with Park. His lazy expression put me at ease immediately. God, he was gorgeous in a way that I never thought I would find attractive. I'd always been turned on by a clean-shaven, suited man that leaned more toward lean than bulky. Park was the complete opposite of that yet I grew wetter with every second that I looked at him.

I broke out of my trance when Park spoke. "I was going to pull out a cheese and cracker platter and engage you in useless chit chat for half an hour before getting down to things. But something tells me you'd be okay skipping that. Am I right?"

My juices had soaked through my panties and were seeping into the crotch of my jeans; that was an answer in itself. "You are right."

Park took my empty wine glass from my hand and placed it on the counter. He reached a hand out to me and I took it. Eagerly. I couldn't wait for Park to cover my body with his naked one. He'd probably suffocate me but what a way to go!

Park pulled me to standing. I barely had my feet under me when he hoisted me up and threw me over his shoulder. My face was upside down looking at Park's lower back. I couldn't stop myself from sticking out my tongue and licking the skin that was so close that I couldn't be expected to resist it. Park responded by swatting my ass hard. The denim took the brunt of the swat but I still felt the sting on my butt cheek. I loved the rush of heat that shot to my pussy, although I didn't need more juices oozing out.

I licked Park's back again, that time squeezing his ass cheeks through his jeans as I did so. I could tell his butt was firm and would be even more impressive naked. Park spanked my ass a second time and another bolt hit me. Damn, he was good.

My foot hit a doorframe as we moved into another room. It didn't hurt but the sound was loud. Park grabbed the back of my thighs and pulled my legs onto his chest. My stomach cut into his shoulder but the sensation was more pleasure than pain. "Keep your arms and legs inside the ride at all times," Park said.

"Cute," I mumbled under my breath, not thinking he would hear me.

"Cute," he repeated, giving my ass its hardest whack yet. "Just a tip - never use the word 'cute' if you want a man to ravage you."

Crap! "My bad." The thought of Park throwing me out of his house without feeling him inside me was horrifying. "Forgive me," I said.

Park didn't answer. "Please," I begged.

Park still didn't answer. "Please," I tried again.

Park flipped me over his shoulder in one swift move. I landed on my back on a bed. But I didn't stay there. Park immediately pulled me to my feet and flung himself onto the bed, leaving me standing at the foot of the mattress. He crossed his arms behind his head and looked at me, a grin on his face that touched his eyes. "I'll forgive you if you strip for me."

Strip? I unknotted my t-shirt and started pulling it upward to yank it over my head. "Stop," Park yelled and I froze. "Strip, I said. Not get undressed. Big difference."

I let go of my shirt and looked at him. I'd never been equally aroused and terrified at the same time. "I'm sorry," I said. "I don't know how to strip." God, that was humiliating to admit.

"Close your eyes." I did it. "Pretend you are alone." That was impossible to do when I was within arm's reach of a hunk but I went with it. "Put your hands on your thighs and slowly run them up your body." I did as he asked. "Slower," he said as my hands passed over my hips.

My hands were moving up my sides when Park said, "Pass slowly over your tits. And grab them."

I ignored the thought that I probably looked ridiculous and kept doing as he said. My nipples hardened when my hands brushed over them. "Pull your hair," Park said, his voice sounding gravely. My fingers went up my neck and dug into my hair. I clenched my fists, my hair threatening to pull out at the roots.

"Move your hands back down your sexy body and slowly pull off your t-shirt." I made my way back down to the bottom of my shirt and started to pull it up. "Slower," Park said.

I felt like I was already going at a snail's pace but I slowed even more. When I had the shirt free of my head, I threw it in the direction of Park's voice, not sure if it hit him.

"Can I open my eyes now?" I asked.

"No. Take off your jeans," Park replied. The button and zipper were still undone so I just needed to take them off. I grabbed the waist of my jeans and was about to slide them down when Park said, "No. Turn around and take them off. Slowly. All the way off."

I turned so I had my back to him. I opened my eyes as I knew Park wouldn't know and took in the part of the room I could see. A dresser sat against the wall directly in front of me. A massive flat screen TV hung on the wall above the dresser. The walls were painted a deep grey, an oddly erotic color. Or maybe I just found the color erotic because I was so turned on.

I slowly worked my jeans down and when I reached my knees, I knew why Park had me turn around; he had a full view of my ass as I bent over to slide my jeans down my calves and off my feet. I dared a quick glance at him through the sliver between my thighs. Seeing the look of lust on his face was worth the risk of opening my eyes. Park looked like he wanted to devour me. Knowing I had that effect on him was a major turn on. It boosted my confidence and I was hit by a wave of assertiveness, something that usually never happened to me in the bedroom.

I slowly stood back up, running my hands up my thighs and over my ass as I did so. I spanked my butt cheek and looked back at Park, putting a finger in my mouth and gnawing on it as I stared at him.

Park was transfixed. I slowly turned so I was facing him and ran my hands over my tits. I cupped my boobs and brushed my nipples through my bra cups. Park's Adam's apple moved as he swallowed deeply.

I turned around and gave him another view of my backside as I reached behind me to undo my bra. When I had it unsnapped, I slowly slid the straps down my arms until the bra fell free of my body. I flung it over my shoulder and it landed in Park's lap. He picked it up and absently caressed my bra as I turned back around, my hands covering my tits.

I bent my head and licked one of my nipples while my hand continued to cover my boob. By the way Park's eyes popped out of his head, I thought he was going to jump off the bed and attack me. The thought of that ramped me up. My pussy was throbbing and screaming for action.

I slid my left hand over so it covered my right boob. The crook in my left arm covered most of my left tit. I slid my right hand down my belly and into my panties. I dove right in, grazing my clit as two of my fingers disappeared into my sloppy pussy. I played around for a minute before pulling my hand out of my core, taking a step closer to Park. I held my wet fingers out toward his mouth.

I thought he would take my fingers between his lips and suck my juices off but I was wrong. He scooted to the end of the bed where I stood, took my hand in his grip, and pushed my fingers toward my face. I opened my mouth and sucked my own juice from my fingers. Damn, I tasted good. When I spit out my fingers, I looked at Park and said, "Delicious. You don't know what you are missing."

His eyes turned dark. I wish I knew what he was thinking. Neither of us moved for many long seconds. Park spoke first. "Take off your panties."

I took a step back and did as he said, my left arm still covering my tits. I left the panties on the carpet and stood, my right hand loosely covering my core.

"Hands to your sides," he said.

I didn't move. "Am I forgiven yet?" I asked.

"Almost. Drop your hands."

I took a deep breath and moved my hands to my waist, standing straight and feigning a confidence I didn't feel.

"Natalie, you are stunning. You have no idea how sexy you are, do you?"

Ignoring his question, I said, "I'm feeling a little overdressed here. Your turn."

Park undid the fly on his jeans and grabbing the bottoms, I slowly started to pull them off. As the pants passed over his hips, his hard cock popped out. "Holy shit," I muttered at the sight of his very impressive boner.

As his jeans cleared his thighs and knees, I asked, "You a fan of commando?"

"The less between my dick and your pussy, the better."

"I love how you think," I replied.

Once I had his jeans off, I tossed them over my shoulder, hearing a thud when they hit the floor.

"Come here," Park said.

I was transfixed by his cock sticking straight up. I couldn't rip my eyes from his crotch area. Still watching his impressive dick, I crawled on all fours up the bed, not stopping until Park and I were face to face. I bent down and kissed him. His mouth opened eagerly, his tongue darting between my teeth even before his lips settled on mine. He devoured my tongue as I moved so my body blanketed his. His cock was poking at my core. I wasn't about to deny either of us for a second longer.

I say upright, reluctantly pulling my lips off his and breaking the kiss. I moved onto my knees and scooted down a couple inches so my thighs book-ended Park's hips. I reached between our bodies and grabbed his shaft, holding his length so he was lined up with my pussy hole. I took a deep breath, silently told myself to stay relaxed, and lowered my body onto his cock.

My body fought his girth at first. I worked hard to remain calm and take him in inch by inch. A long minute passed before he was buried all the way inside me. I'd never had a man as large as Park and it felt like he was touching me everywhere.

Park curled his fingers around my hips and tried to prod me upward. "Give me a second," I said.

Park let go of my hips. His hands moved to my tits where he busied himself with the playground on my chest. I barely registered the titty play; I was too focused on what was going on inside me.

Once my pussy had adjusted to Park's girth, I started to slowly move up and down his shaft. I loved how full I felt with him inside me, threatening to tickle my tonsils from the inside.

Park's hands returned to my hips and he again tried to get me to move faster. I was in a lazier mood than he was, wanting to take my time and enjoy every moment of Park's girth. But he was having none of that. When he saw that his attempts to get me to go faster were futile, he wrapped his arms around my back, pressed our chests together, and did a barrel roll. When we stopped moving, I was lying on the bed and Park was on top of me.

I let out a squeal but had no other chance to react before Park reared back and drove his cock into me. Hard. And harder the second time. He was moving so fast that he was a blur. I closed my eyes and lay my head back against the bed, overwhelmed by the sensations flowing through me as Park rammed into me over and over again. He hit my g-spot almost every time his cock slid into me, something I wasn't used to. Not that I was complaining! It caused another orgasm to build at a rapid pace and I knew it wouldn't be long until I came again. Damn, Park was good. Danny hadn't been exaggerating.

I dug my hands into my hair and tugged, the feeling of pain somehow helping me keep control. Just when I thought I was going to dissolve into a cesspool of horniness-induced euphoria, Park reached into my core and ravaged my clit with his fingertips. Between that and the g-spot massage his cock was giving me, I exploded.

I had to work hard to stay conscious as my mind and body were deluged by ecstasy. My climax tore through me, robbing me of the ability to do anything. I heard Park speak as if through a tin can, mumbling something about squeezing or milking. His hands were back on my chest but I couldn't register what they were doing. I couldn't move, I couldn't think, I could barely breathe. I had no choice but to lay there and soak up the ribbons of release coursing through me. I was in erotic heaven.

I wasn't sure if minutes or hours passed before I was able to crack one eye open. Park was still above me, his torso filling most of my field of vision. "You okay?" he asked as he smoothed a lock of my hair off my face. "That seemed intense."

I nodded, not trusting that I had the ability to speak yet.

Park said, "Good. Because now I really want to fuck you good."

I thought he'd fucked me pretty damn good moments ago! A part of me was hesitant of what was to come if that had been a mediocre fucking I'd just been on the receiving end of.

Park pulled me into his arms and my legs instinctively wrapped around his waist. His hard cock was pressing against my pelvic bone as we walked out of the bedroom. A bolt of lust shot through me. Hot damn, how could I want him so intensely again when moments ago I'd had two of the best orgasms I've had in years. I didn't question it; I just ground my body against his cock as another wave of desire hit me.

My ass landed with a thud on top of the kitchen counter. Grabbing my thigh, Park pulled me so my butt hung over the edge. I was about to teeter off but Park stopped me before my legs fell down to the floor. He took a second to look between my legs as he lined up his cock. "You have a perfect pussy, Natalie." He drove into me and I felt like I'd been rammed by a bull. Park's hands moved to my hips, clutching them tight so his thrusts didn't drive me back onto the counter. "Oh yeah," he groaned. "This is what I like. Squeeze me baby!"

He was already tight inside me but I clenched my pussy walls around him. "Yeah, baby. More," Park said.

I kept tightening around his cock, getting a kick out of the way his eyes glazed over and his tongue rested on his teeth.

Park said, "You are so hot. Play with your tits."

I took a boob in each hand and tweaked my nipples as he watched me. His driving force kicked up a notch and he grunted with each thrust. I was so wet that I must've been oozing onto his countertop. His eyes never left my chest as I continued squeezing his dick and playing with my tits. I could feel another orgasm building but my focus was on watching Park; seeing his pleasure was the greatest turn on imaginable.

Park kept going, like a human version of the Energizer Bunny. My lower back was sore from the hard counter but I ignored it; it would've taken a category ten earthquake to get me to move from that spot.

"Want to watch me cum?" Park asked, his voice husky.

"Shit yeah," I said, figuring his blow would be impressive.

"You gonna cum soon?"

My orgasm had been building but I wasn't close yet. "No, I need a few minutes."

"I can't wait that long."

"I'm good. I want to watch you explode."

Park stood back and pulled his massive cock out of me, giving it two last pumps with his hand as he shot his jism all over my body. It went everywhere. Gobs of it landed on my tits and slid down into the valley between them. Some pooled in the divot at the base of my throat while more ended up on my belly. A trail of Park's jism went from my stomach to my crotch, a few drops hiding in my trimmed pubic hair. Some was still oozing out of his cock as he shoved my legs apart. With his hands flat on my inner thighs, he pushed me further up the counter, stopping when my knees were at the edge and my feet hung down toward the floor. Without warning, his face dove into my core and his tongue began a pleasure assault on my pussy. I rested my head back on the counter, closed my eyes, and basked in the joy of being eaten out by someone who knows what he is doing.

I heard Park rifling through a drawer under the counter I was on but he never lost his focus on pussy chowing. My orgasm flared back up and continued to build. After the drawer rummaging stopped, I felt something besides Park's tongue and fingers in my pussy area. It was hard, like plastic. Park's tongue moved from my pussy lips to my clit as the hard object circled my core. As Park's tongue picked up speed, the hard thing slid into my pussy. It went slowly at first. When I didn't stop Park, he moved the thing with more speed, not just in and out but also swirling it around. The swirling was a strange sensation but an intensely pleasurable one as it hit my sensitive parts deep inside.

Under Park's expert tongue, my orgasm steadily grew. I challenged myself to hold it at bay as long as possible, knowing it would be even more intense when it hit. But my attempts didn't even make a dent in slowing it down.

I leaned up a bit so I could dig my fingers into Park's hair. I thought my head rubbing would distract him and slow his tongue but I was wrong; touching him spurred him on even more. I gave into the inevitable and let orgasm #3 hit me.

Typically my successive orgasms weren't as powerful as the one before it but the one that barrelled through me moments later was as powerful as the first one had been. I screamed Park's name, more out of gratitude for the gift his tongue gave me than anything else. A bunch of gibberish followed but as I was still climaxing, I had no clue what I'd said. Not that I cared - my pussy and my body were so happy and content that I felt like climbing to the top of the closest mountain and singing *Kumbaya*.

When I could move, I slowly sat up and looked at Park. "Anyone ever tell you that you are amazing?" I asked him.

Park just smiled at me, either too humble or too well mannered to answer my question. He took my hand and helped me off the counter. He had a spatula in his other hand and I bust out laughing. "Is that what was in me?"

"Sure was. I'll never make another grilled cheese sandwich without thinking of you."

"Well, I'm honored."

"And you are beautiful. And a lot of fun. I had a great time tonight with you."

"Me, too. Thanks for having me over." I collected my clothes from various places around Park's house and redressed. When I had everything, I gave Park a kiss on the cheek and said, "Seriously, thanks for this. You have no idea how much I needed it."

"Happy to help."

Park opened his front door. I stepped into the night and made my way to my Honda, trying to sashay as I could feel Park still watching me. I started my car, threw Park one last wave, and headed home. Once there, I collapsed into a dreamless coma-like sleep, my body more blissful than it had been in years.

#####

I was late for work the next morning. I must've shut off my alarm and fallen back asleep although I didn't remember doing so. I blamed it on Park and his lovemaking skills that I couldn't get out of bed until after ten. I slithered into my desk around eleven and Danny's head popped into my workspace seconds later. "Hey, I covered for you. I told Doris that you had a meeting outside of the office this morning. I told her you must've forgotten to put it in your calendar. I knew you would be late today if Park was on his game last night."

I finally glanced up at and looked at Danny, the movement requiring a ridiculous amount of strength. "Thanks for covering for me. You guessed right - Park was on his game last night."

"Lucky you."

"Yes."

"We still on for tonight?" he asked.

"Of course. I wouldn't bail on you."

"I wasn't sure you'd be able to physically handle it after last night."

"I'll be fine," I assured him. "It's nothing a quick nap before I pick you up won't cure."

"Still have my address?'

"Of course."

"Okay. I'll see you at 8:45."

"I'll be there. And hey, thanks again for covering for me this morning."

"No problem."

I tried to focus on work but it was impossible. All I could think about was the fun I'd had with Park and the night ahead at The Swinger's Club. I had no idea what to expect and it was that unknown factor that was the most exciting part.

#####

I arrived at Danny's townhome at 8:45 sharp. He must've been watching for me as less than ten seconds later, he opened my passenger door. "Good evening," he said as he slid inside.

I let out a whistle. "Hot stuff," I said, impressed by how dashing he looked in his tailored suit and collarless shirt. "You clean up pretty damn good." I would've never guessed that Danny could look so attractive.

"You look great yourself," Danny said. While his words were obligatory after what I'd said, I could tell by the way his eyes lingered on my body that he meant it. Not that I cared what Danny's opinion was of me. Other than needing a male figure with me for tonight, Danny was a nonentity in my life.

That aside, I knew I looked good tonight. I'd taken extra care doing my hair and makeup and my simple black dress hinted at what lay underneath in an understated yet sexy way.

As I pulled away from the curb, I said, "Thanks again for doing this with me."

"It's my pleasure. I'm happy to help," Danny replied as he wiped his hands on his pressed pants.

"You nervous?" I asked

Danny laughed. "Does it show?"

"Only a little."

"It's strange going somewhere knowing you are going to have to perform sexually. That's a lot of pressure on a man."

I patted his arm. "You'll be fine. Just try and have fun."

"Easy for you to say. You're a woman. You can fake it if you have to and no one would know."

"Don't stress, Danny. We'll find you a sexy creature and your body will do its thing."

"I hope you're right."

"I am."

I found the club easily and pulled into the first parking spot I could find. The parking lot was huge and it was almost full. The Swinger's Club was clearly a rocking place to be on a Friday night.

I locked my purse and coat in my trunk - I didn't need them for the next two hours - and took Danny's arm. "We're going to have so much fun. I promise you're going to be kneeling down and kissing my feet to thank me by the time we leave," I said as we cut through rows of cars lined up like soldiers.

Danny laughed, this time more a sound of relief than nervousness. "I hope you are right."

"I already know I am. Now smile," I ordered.

Danny plastered on a cartoonish fake grin as he opened the door to the club and let me go in before him. The lady in the foyer checked our names off against her list, wished us a pleasant evening, and directed us into the club.

The place was huge. I could barely see from one end to the other, it was that long. Danny looked overwhelmed. "Now what?" he asked me. He looked ready to panic and bolt. I couldn't blame him, the place was cavernous.

"Let's go get a drink."

The place had bars lined along every wall. I bypassed the first few sections as the bartenders were busy. Halfway into the space, I spotted a lady on the other side of the bar who was working hard to stifle a yawn. I pointed Danny in her direction.

"How can I help you?" she asked us, clearly thrilled to have customers.

"I'll have a mojito please. What would you like?" I asked Danny. When he didn't say anything, I looked in his direction. He still stood beside me although his back was to the bartender. He was staring at something in the middle of the room, his mouth sagging open as he paid me no attention. I knew he was a beer guy so I turned back to the bartender and said, "He'll have a beer. Whatever you have on tap is fine."

"Coming right up."

While she busied herself getting our drinks, I asked Danny, "You okay?"

He nodded slowly, his mouth still gaping open.

"What is it?" I asked.

"I. Found. Her."

"Her?"

"The woman I can get it up for without a worry."

"Who?" There were hundreds of women in the room.

"That one over there in the red pantsuit catsuit thing. Whatever you call those outfits."

"Pantsuit works. Big brown hair and lots of cleavage?"

"That's her."

I paid the bartender, handed Danny his beer, grabbed my mojito, and said, "Follow me."

Before Danny could stop me, I made a beeline for his dream woman. "Sorry to bother you. I was hoping you could help me."

The woman gave me her full attention and I saw she was even more beautiful up close than she looked from across the room. "Shoot."

"This is the first time we've been here," I said, head nodding to Danny who really needed to close his gaping mouth. "We're not sure how it works."

"Well, first of all, welcome. My name is Veronica."

"Thank you. I'm Natalie. This is Danny." We all shook hands, Danny's lingering longer in Veronica's than mine did.

Veronica said, "It's pretty simple. You keep looking until you find another couple you are both interested in. When all four of you agree, the opposite man and lady go off to private rooms." Veronica pointed to the second level. "The private rooms are up there."

"What if you don't find a couple you connect with?" I asked.

"That's impossible. Look at the number of people here. Unless you are looking for something humanly unattainable, you'll be able to find another pair that all of you are happy with."

"Fair enough."

Danny finally spoke, "Are you available? I want you."

Veronica cast him a look that I couldn't decipher. "I'll chalk your bluntness up to this being your first time here. My partner, Kyle, and I haven't been spoken for this evening yet. So we'll see."

"We'll see what?" Danny asked. He could be such a dunce.

"Kyle should be back any minute. Once he gets here, we'll have a chat and take it from there. We'll see if we all like each other and want to take it to private rooms."

"Thank you for the details," I said. "We probably stick out as newbies."

"Nonsense," Veronica replied. "It's always nice to have newcomers join us."

Danny was about to say something when Veronica said, "Ah, here he is now. Kyle, I'd like to introduce you to Natalie and Danny."

I turned and came face-to-face with the sexiest silver fox I'd ever seen. He was probably in his early 30s but he'd been greying for years. It looked sexy on him and didn't distract from the body that was obviously buff under his pants and button-down shirt. My eyes were drawn to his trim waist that a belt with a sleek silver buckle accented nicely. "Natalie," he said, my name sounding like velvet as it rolled out from between his lips.

"That's me. Kyle?"

"You got it," he replied as he stuck out his hand.

I slid my palm into his and knew when we touched that I would be fucking him like a stallion within the hour. His sex appeal was understated but bubbling below the surface, waiting to be released.

Kyle let go of my hand and turned his attention to Danny. As they exchanged introductions, I studied Kyle's profile. I would probably pass him on the street without looking twice but here, in this environment, he was the guy for me. My time with Park had proven that I needed to step out of my comfort zone when it came to my bedmates.

Veronica asked me a question but I hadn't been paying attention. "I'm sorry, what was that?" I asked.

"Shall we have a seat?"

"Sure."

Danny and I followed Veronica and Kyle to a long bench that had enough empty space for the four of us.

Veronica motioned for Danny to sit at the end. He did so eagerly, like a puppy desperate to please. I sat next to her and Kyle sat on the other side of me.

A wave of imbalance hit me and I started to babble, my default mode when nerves took over. "So, you come here often?" I asked Kyle.

Before he could answer, I continued, "Sorry. That was rude. You don't have to answer. This is my first time here, my first time trying swinging actually, so I don't really know what I'm doing. Okay, I'll stop talking now. I'm so sorry."

Kyle put a hand on my knee. Most of his hand was on my dress but where two of his fingers lay on the skin below my hem, a fire burst to life. I glanced down to see if I needed to drop and roll to put out the flames. I was actually stunned that my skin wasn't burning.

I looked at Kyle's face and we made real eye contact for the first time. Holy shit - his square jaw and blue eyes that pierced into mine were the ribbon on a perfect package. "Take a breath," Kyle said.

He waited until I inhaled and exhaled before he continued, "There's nothing to be nervous about. This is fun. It can be a lot of fun if you let it. Trust me."

"What do we do now?" I asked.

"We chat a bit while Veronica and your guy chat. Then we decide if we want to go upstairs to private rooms or move on and find other couples to hook up with."

I didn't need to say another word to Kyle to know that I wanted to be naked and writhing underneath him. But I would play along until we were alone.

"Tell me about yourself, Natalie," Kyle said.

"Well, I'm 25-years-old. I work in the IT department of an HR company. I'm a bit of a geek so I like to write code and read books in my free time. And swim and hike. I like nature."

"You are the sexiest geek I have ever met."

"Well, thank you," I said as I blushed a fiery red from my neck up to my hairline. "Tell me about you."

"I like to hike and swim, too. And extreme camping. I used to be in the marines but I retired a few years ago to start my own company."

"What kind of company?"

"Private security. We mainly train men and women to work security for VIPs."

"Wow. That's cool. What was it like being in the marines?"

"I liked it. It allowed me to serve my country, something I felt strongly that I needed to do."

His time in the military explained the hunky body. "Not much of a leap from the marines to security, is it?"

"Not too much."

Something over my shoulder caught Kyle's attention. He put a hand back on my knee and said, "One second." It was a good thing he was looking past me as I knew I had a goofy look on my face as my body turned to mush under his touch. Good God, if he could melt me with a couple of fingers, I'd probably pass out when his whole body was pleasuring me.

I felt a tap on my shoulder. I looked up to see Danny standing beside me. "Veronica and I are taking off. Are you good?"

"More than good. Have fun."

"You, too." Danny bent down and whispered in my ear, "Thanks for bringing me tonight."

"No problem. Now get going," I said as Veronica was halfway to the stairway already.

I turned back toward Kyle. Relief flooded through me when I realized what was happening - we were about to be alone. Alone and naked!

"Shall we?" Kyle asked.

"I'd love to."

Kyle kept his hand on the small of my back as we walked toward the stairs. It took every ounce of strength to keep putting one foot in front of the other as my focus was obliterated thanks to Kyle's touch.

Kyle took my elbow as we climbed the stairs to the second level. I wondered if he knew I needed the support to keep from melting into a puddle at his feet.

Once we reached the second floor, I followed Kyle until he stopped in front of a door with a *vacant* sign on it. He flipped the sign over so it read *occupied.* "After you," he said, gesturing me inside.

I stepped into a room that was probably 12 x 12. It wasn't a big space but it didn't need to be as the only furniture was a bed and a chair. When Kyle closed the door, the loud click caused me to jump.

Kyle came to where I stood. "Let's see if we can get you to relax," he said.

He rested his hands on my shoulders and slowly began kneading them, rubbing the tension out. He didn't rush, he moved as if we had all the time in the world.

His thumbs went to work on my shoulder blades, somehow separating the bones from the knots that surrounded them. When I groaned out loud, a sound that could probably be categorized as a human purr, Kyle said, "Lay down so I can get the rest of your back."

With his superpower fingers, I wasn't going to refuse that offer. I dropped face first into the middle of the bed. I heard Kyle shuffling his clothes before he moved onto the bed, his legs on either side of my hips. His hands moved to my back and he steamrolled over every speck of tension. I was melting more into the bed with every touch.

Kyle said, "Can I undo your zipper?" I knew he meant the zipper that ran from the back of my neck to the top of my butt.

"Please." I was eager to feel his hands directly on my flesh.

He unzipped me at snail speed, the cool air kissing my heated skin and making me break out in goose bumps. His hands slid into the gap, one palm cupping each side of my ribcage. The touch was so erotic that my body reacted violently, my arms moving harshly against my sides, pinning Kyle's hands in place. When he tried to pull his hands free, I squeezed my arms tighter. "Give me one second," I said. I took a half dozen deep breaths before I made myself loosen my grip and move my arms up so my body made a "T" on the bed.

Kyle's hands continued circling my ribs, not stopping until each of his hands cupped a breast. Despite my chest being pressed into the bed, Kyle was able to grab a handful of each tit.

He bent down and said into my ear, "I want to suck your nipples. Roll over."

That was the best idea I'd heard all day. Once Kyle pulled his hands free of my dress, I rolled over, sliding the top of my dress down to my waist. I wasn't wearing a bra as one was built into the dress so I was naked from my waist up.

Kyle grabbed an ankle and pulled me so I was sitting on the edge of the bed. He nudged my legs apart as he kneeled on the floor between them and buried his face in my tits.

Holy shit! Kyle made love to my chest, there was no other way to describe it. He sucked and fondled and tweaked my boobs until they were physically aching in the best possible way. My nipples had never stuck out so far from my body, as if they were trying to jut their way into Kyle's mouth for more action.

My core was on fire from the copious amount of tit action. It amazed me how there was a direct line from my nipples to my pussy; when my nips were pleasured, my pussy throbbed and grew wet. I was more than ready for Kyle to bury himself in me.

In lieu of saying, "Screw me," I reached between our bodies, my hand in search of his cock. As I couldn't bend down because his face was in my chest, I only managed to graze the top of his boxer shorts. (He'd ditched his pants when I'd fallen onto the bed and was now only wearing his shirt and boxers.)

Kyle pulled his face away from my tits. "Looking for something?" he asked.

"I sure am. Your cock."

"Is someone a little eager? We have lots of time."

"Patience isn't my strong suit when I'm horny."

"Fair enough. What would you like?"

"I'd like you inside me."

"Every heard of foreplay?" he asked.

What the hell was with all the conversation? I didn't come here for chitchat. "I'm fine to keep foreplay to a minimum."

Kyle stood and unbuttoned his shirt as he looked down at me. "I like a woman who knows what she wants." He paused as his eyes devoured me. "What are you waiting for?" he asked. "Get naked so I can give you what you want."

I shimmied my dress down my hips and kicked it off my body, leaving me in only thigh high stockings and a thong.

As Kyle looked at me, his hard-on flexed inside his boxers, a beacon to a woman who wanted to be sexually ravaged. I sat up and grabbed the waistband of his shorts, yanking them down his legs as I made sure to hold them open far enough so they wouldn't catch on his boner. Kyle stepped out of the boxers as he tossed his shirt to the side.

Kyle finally naked, I was able to admire his body. Had I not known it previously, it would've been obvious that he got his physique from doing real-life work, not from a gym. His chest was wide and his shoulders bulged. His waist was tiny in comparison; the muscles around his abs looked like they were sculpted out of marble. He flared back out at the hip, a torso made for fucking. He could probably go for hours with all the power in those hips, something I was looking forward to being on the receiving end of.

Kyle put a hand on my shoulder and shoved me back so I was lying on the bed. He reached between my legs and grabbed my thong, yanking it off my body with the effort it would take to brush away a fly. He tossed the tiny swatch of material over his shoulder and pounced onto the bed between my spread and bent knees. I was so ready for him that I could almost feel the relief already.

Kyle grabbed his cock with one hand as his other hand slid from the top of my knee down to my thigh. His fingers slid under my stocking, his touch leaving a trail of fire. He squeezed the flesh of my thigh hard, a thrill running from one end of the limb to the other. My other leg curled up to wrap around his waist, pulling him toward me.

He took the hint and I'd never been so grateful for anything in my life. He slid the head of his cock into me and my body went wild, trying desperately to pull him in the rest of the way.

I ripped my gaze from where I'd been watching Kyle's cock disappear into me and looked at his face. "What are you waiting for?" I challenged him, working hard to soften my words as I knew my frustration was showing through. And that was never attractive.

"Just making sure you are ready," Kyle said.

"I'm more than ready." My foot on the small of his back was trying to pull him toward me. I felt him give in to my urging, his cock starting to slowly slide into me.

"Oh yeah, that's it," I said, my pussy stretching to accommodate his girth. "Keep going," I begged. I knew I should be grateful that I was finally getting what I wanted but the only thing I could focus on was that I wanted him faster.

He was almost all the way into my depths when we both froze as someone knocked at the door. "Who could that be?" I whispered.

"No clue. I'll go check. Maybe there's an emergency?"

It took every ounce of my strength to remove my leg from Kyle's waist and let it fall onto the bed. Kyle pushed off me and my frustration level ramped up a dozen notches. I was so horny I was ready to go mount the doorknob.

Keeping his body behind the door, Kyle opened it a few inches. A guy who looked like a young Arnold Schwarzenegger stood on the other side. Arnie mumbled something I couldn't quite make out. Kyle replied by opening the door wider and looking at me as he said, "That's fine with me but you'll have to ask the lady here."

"You mind if I watch?" Arnie asked me.

I must've had a look of confusion on my face as he continued, "I'll sit in the chair and be quiet. You won't even know I'm here."

I looked at Kyle and said, "That's fine with me if it's good with you." Whatever it took to get Kyle back to this bed to finish what he started.

Kyle opened the door all the way, let Arnie inside, and closed the door behind him. Kyle resumed his spot between my legs as Arnie sat in the chair. Arnie looked closer to my age than Kyle's in his jeans and pressed t-shirt. The eagerness in his eyes was hard to ignore. It looked like we'd made his day by letting him in. Well, we probably did.

"Ready?" Kyle asked.

"Stop asking. You know I am."

He rammed his cock into me without a primer. I closed my eyes and flung my hands out to my sides as my body embraced his poundings. "Thank you," I whispered under my breath so no one could hear me. Tears tickled the back of my eyelids as relief and lust coursed through me.

I'd been so worked up that an orgasm raced toward me at Mach speeds. I grabbed Kyle's ass, one cheek in each of my hands, and pulled him harder into me with every thrust. Just before my orgasm hit, I wrapped my legs around his waist, opening my core even more so he got deeper inside me. "Shit yeah," I screamed as I climaxed, my fingers digging into his ass. One of my nails pierced his skin but I couldn't let go. My body was completely obliterated by the sexual tsunami that had wiped me out.

Kyle didn't stop as my body continued to peak. My arms fell to my sides but my legs stayed around him, my ankles locked behind his back. I tuned Kyle out and solely focused on the chaos going on inside me. I was in heaven and I was in no rush to leave.

It pained me that all good things came to an end. I returned to reality and Kyle was still plunging into me over and over. His cock caressed my insides, rubbing my sensitive bits. I lifted my arms off the bed and ran them up and down Kyle's broad back.

A movement from the side of my eye caught my attention. I glanced over to see Arnie still sitting in the chair, his cock in his hand. He was slowly stroking himself as he watched Kyle fuck me, his eyes as big as coffee mugs. I stuck one of my fingers in my mouth and sucked it as I looked straight at Arnie. His eyes bugged out even further and his self-stroking speed jacked up a few degrees.

"Hey," Kyle said and I turned to look at him.

"Yeah?" I replied.

"You losing interest in me already?"

"Not at all." No part of me could forget what Kyle's cock was doing to me, that was impossible. "I'm just throwing the guy a bone."

By the way Kyle's lips tightened as he looked down at me, I could've sworn he was jealous. Instead of saying something, Kyle pulled out of me, grabbed the tops of my outer thighs, and savagely flipped me over. He slapped my ass hard three times before plunging into me from behind, driving me up the bed. I moved a few inches each time he thrust into my depths, my body not stopping until my skull hit the velvety headboard. I love angry sex. I loved when a guy was pissy and took it out by pounding a woman even harder.

I knew I was being tempestuous when I picked my head up off the bed and glanced back over my left shoulder at Arnie. When I threw him a lecherous grin as I watched him whacking his long cock, Kyle reacted instantly. He grabbed a handful of my hair and yanked my head back. As the strands threatened to pull out of my scalp, a bolt of electricity shot to my core. Along with angry sex, I loved sexual pain. I got off on it. I hadn't yet found a man that gave me enough lusty pain so I relished every torturous touch when I was on the receiving end of it.

So did my pussy. It started contracting wildly, squeezing Kyle's cock so tight that I wouldn't have been surprised if he'd burst into a dozen pieces inside me.

Kyle groaned, a guttural sound an animal would make. He let go of my hair, pulled his cock out of me, and rested his forehead on my back. "Christ, Natalie, you are a handful. I don't want to cum yet."

"Then don't." I rolled out from under him and beelined for Arnie. "Don't go anywhere, Kyle. I'll give you a second to catch your breath before round two."

Arnie looked panicked as I approached him. "Relax," I said. "You'll like this, I promise."

The chair he sat in had no arms. I stepped over him so one of my legs was on either side of the chair, Arnie's thighs between me. Arnie let go of his cock to grab at my tits, which were shoved in his face from my positioning. Not that he seemed to mind. After he got over his initial shock, Arnie attacked my boobs with his lips, taking both of my nipples in his mouth at the same time. He bit down on them too hard but the pain kicked me up a notch on the horniness scale.

I took a firm grip of Arnie's cock and held it straight up. I sank down onto his shaft, my pussy thrilled to have someone inside her to play with again. Arnie's cock didn't have much girth but he made up for it in length; he was so long that he touched places in me that had never been reached before. "Oh yeah, that's it," I said once he was fully in me.

Arnie kept playing with my tits as I started to ride him. His entire body shuddered. I looked at his face to make sure he was okay. The expression on his face was probably identical to what Park had seen on my face last night. I had total confidence that Arnie was more than good to go.

I picked up my riding pace, intending to get off on Arnie before returning to Kyle. If Kyle got me off one more time after I was done with Arnie, that would give me a total of three orgasms for the night; I would leave here a very happy woman.

I moved my hands to Arnie's shoulder, using them as leverage to hold me steady as I rode him even faster. His cock was hitting some unusual places inside me. While it felt amazing, I knew my body well enough to know that I could keep going as I was and it would take hours for me to cum. I scooted a fraction closer to Arnie so the side of his cock brushed my clit every time I sank down onto him. That worked - an orgasm ignited, starting a slow burn to what would eventually be a breath-stealing eruption.

I'd closed my eyes and was lost in the bliss of riding a hard cock when I felt Arnie freeze. His mouth and hands left my tits suddenly, a strange sensation after their relentless playing. I opened my eyes to see what was going on and the first thing I noticed was a look of trepidation on Arnie's face. He was looking over my shoulder at something that clearly made him nervous.

I knew a second later that it was Kyle approaching us that had Arnie trembling. Kyle's hands rested on my shoulders for a brief second before sliding down to cup my breasts. He held one in each hand, weighing them as if they were juggling balls. His still-hard cock poked into my back, reminding me how great it felt when Kyle anger-fucked me. He was probably pretty pissed off right now, if the fierce way he was mashing my tits was any indication.

Kyle whispered, "Fuck this," under his breath. I probably wasn't supposed to hear him but I did. I was about to turn around and ask him if he was okay when his hands moved from my tits down to my waist, his arms circling me. He yanked me off Arnie and spun me in a circle. He threw me across the room where I landed in a heap on the bed. I screamed in surprise as my pussy flooded with juice; men who took charge turned me on big time.

Kyle followed me onto the bed less than a second later. I lay on my back as he towered over me, his face a mask of anger and lust. I didn't know what to say or do so I stayed still and threw him a tiny smile.

Whispering so Arnie couldn't hear him, Kyle asked, "Did you like the pencil dick fucking you?" He slid a hand between my legs and shoved a couple fingers in me. "Hell, one of my fingers is bigger than what that kids' got."

I thought this would be the wrong moment to have the debate over whether size or knowing how to use it is better. Instead, I closed my eyes and surrendered to the waves of pleasure that were going through me thanks to Kyle's fingers. The guy sure knew how to touch a woman's intimate parts, I'd give him that.

The climax that had sparked to life when I was sitting on Arnie rapidly grew closer each time Kyle hit my g-spot or clit with his thumb or fingers. "Yeah, that's how I like it" I said, hoping he'd keep his hand in my core until I came. "That feels amazing."

The orgasm raced toward me. I let it come, literally, embracing it even before it arrived. I could feel Kyle's hand start slowing down as I was about to pass the point of no return. I panicked, not wanting to lose a climax that was so close. "Don't stop," I begged. "I'm about to cum."

Kyle put me out of my sexual misery and picked up his finger fucking speed. "Yes," I screamed as I exploded, my relief tangible. "Yes, yes, yes," I moaned.

Kyle kept his fingers in me as I continued to peak, although he stopped moving them. My overstimulated pussy was grateful as she needed a minute to recover.

Kyle's hard cock nudging at the top of my inner thigh brought me back to the realization that I wasn't the only one with needs. I lifted my legs from where they'd melted into the bed and wrapped them around Kyle's waist. He pulled his hand out of my core and settled between my thighs, his cock prodding at my pussy. Again so quiet that Arnie couldn't hear, Kyle said, "I'm going to make you regret leaving me to go to pencil dick."

I risked a glance over at Arnie. He was still in the chair, slowly stroking himself. Giving my full attention back to Kyle, I said, "Do it."

He drove into me, filling every crevice. My eyes rolled back into my head as Kyle's cock attacked me with a vengeance I'd never experienced before. My body embraced it, my pussy challenging Kyle to give me even more. Kyle stepped up his game when he grabbed two pillows from the top of the bed, lifted me up, shoved the pillows under my backside, and dropped me so my ass lay on the clouds of fluff. He tossed my legs over his shoulders, wrapped his large hands around my hipbones, and drove into me. With the pillows under me and my legs in the air, Kyle angled into me in a way that got him even deeper than before. My body was on fire from the inside out, another orgasm rapidly building.

I didn't think I would cum again so soon but with Kyle fucking me like he was doing judo on my pussy, I knew it wouldn't take long. When one of his hands let go of my hip to rub my clit, I was done for. My already swollen nub flooded under Kyle's touch, kicking up my orgasm's approach. I screamed out again as I came, my body overloaded like never before. I had never climaxed so many times so close together and my body was clueless as to how to cope. Sure, I've cum more than three times in one night but never within what felt like minutes. I focused on taking slow, deep breaths as I absorbed every nuance Kyle's cock imparted in me.

I felt him move off me but I didn't open my eyes or acknowledge him. I knew I'd have to focus on his cock when I could function again but I needed another minute to get my strength back.

When I was able to move, I cracked open my eyes to see Kyle standing at the end of the bed. He was looking at me as he stroked his cock. He grabbed one of my ankles and pulled me to the edge of the bed. He didn't do anything else, just looked at me as he played with himself. I didn't know if I should sit up and suck his dick or stay where I was; I opted to remain still until Kyle told me otherwise since it was all about him now.

Kyle looked over his shoulder at Arnie cemented in the chair. Kyle threw him a 'come here' head nod and after hesitating for a moment, Arnie joined Kyle at the end of the bed. Both of them stood jerking themselves as they looked down at me.

Kyle came first, shooting an impressive amount of cum over my chest and thighs. As his stream slowed down, I sat up and took him in my mouth, sucking the last of his jism from his cock. Kyle dug his hands into my hair as my lips slowly pumped him, pulling my hair tight as my mouth Hoovered him. I didn't stop until he started to soften. Only then did I gently push him out of my mouth. He let go of my hair and collapsed face first onto the bed beside me.

I turned my attention to Arnie. He was still standing and stroking his cock. I pushed his hand aside and took his cock into my mouth. His hand moved to my shoulder where it dug into my flesh as my lips sealed tight around his shaft. "Fuck," he slurred as he exploded in my mouth even before my lips had a chance to stroke him. His cum shot my tonsils, covering them with his hot, sticky jism. My mouth almost filled up before he was doze oozing out.

I sucked every drop off Arnie's cock, not letting go of him until his legs started to buckle. My mouth released his cock and he stumbled backward, falling into the chair.

I fell onto the bed beside Kyle, my arms flailing out. One hit Kyle's back and I mindlessly rubbed the muscles that his skin barely managed to contain. Kyle was definitely built for pleasuring a woman.

The first one to move was Arnie. He threw on his clothes as if the place was on fire, his fly barely zipped up before he opened the door. He threw us a, "Thanks," before leaving the room, the door slamming behind him.

I looked over at Kyle and smiled. "That was fun," I said.

"Sure was. But you had me going with that kid for a minute there."

"He wasn't a kid, he was probably my age."

"He looked twelve."

"True." I took a deep breath as my eyes studied Kyle's body, memorizing as much of him as I could for when I wanted to reminisce about this amazing night.

"Now what?" I asked.

"We put our clothes back on and go find Veronica and Danny."

I playfully swatted at Kyle and he did the same, pushing me off the bed. I laughed as I hit the floor, glad this rendezvous was ending on a comical note.

We both rounded up our clothes and redressed. "Ready?" I asked when we both looked decent.

"Hold on." Kyle cupped my face with his hands and kissed me, stopping just before things were about to get heated again. "Thank you for a great night," he said. "I haven't had this much fun in a long time."

"No, thank YOU. That was unforgettable."

Kyle let go of me. I opened the door and he swatted my ass as I stepped into the hallway.

We spotted Veronica and Danny as we descended the stairs. Danny looked like he'd just won the sexual lottery. I probably had the same look on my face.

We parted ways once the four of us connected. As Danny and I walked out to my car, he said, "Wow. That was the best night of my life. Let me know if you ever need a date to go again. I'm your man."

"I'm sure I'll take you up on that generous offer. I can't imagine not having another night of lusty pleasure at The Swinger's Club."

#####

I hope you enjoyed The Swinger's Club quadrilogy!
Follow me on Twitter @ZoeWaters13
Email me at zoewaters13@gmail.com

To read more of my books, check out an online retailer. My list of titles includes:
Romp at the Reunion
One Night of Lust
Stroke of Kismet
Virginity For Sale
One Night of Swinging
Swapping Spouses
Lover Under Covers
Airport Rendezvous
Seduced by Fire
Swapping Spouses: The Other Couple
Out of Bounds
Swapping Spouses: The Aftermath
A Life Restarted
Lover Under Covers: Second Assignment
The Others
Swapping Spouses: One Year Later
Out of Bounds: The Pick Up
Another Night of Swinging
Arranged
Protecting the Princess
The House Sitter
72 Hours: Pick Your Erotic Adventure
Ghost of Love: Life and Death Erotica
Then Came the Prince

Modern Lust: 3 Erotic Shorts
Swinging Spouses
Swinging Spouses: Round Two
Swinging Spouses: Round Three
Swinging Spouses: Round Four
The Swinger's Club: Tiffany and Liam
The Swinger's Club: Chad and Lexi
The Swinger's Club: Amanda Worthington
The Swinger's Club: Natalie Smyth

Have a great day!
Zoe
Xoxoxo

Printed in Great Britain
by Amazon

32167879R00104